POSI PIRATES

Share D'All

MAPLE
PUBLISHERS

Positive Pirates

Author: Share D'All

Copyright © Share D'All (2022)

The right of Share D'All to be identified as author of this work has been asserted by the author in accordance with section 77 and 78 of the Copyright, Designs and Patents Act 1988.

First Published in 2022

ISBN 978-1-915164-02-5 (Paperback)
    978-1-915164-03-2 (Ebook)

Cover Design and Book Layout by:

White Magic Studios
www.whitemagicstudios.co.uk

Published by:

Maple Publishers
1 Brunel Way,
Slough,
SL1 1FQ, UK
www.maplepublishers.com

CONTENTS

Chapter 1: Setting the Scene

Our story takes place over two hundred years ago when some things about life were quite different. People still had thoughts and feelings the same as we do, but there were even more things they didn't understand.

The idea of science was very new, and most people had never heard of it, which meant things we take for granted now were a mystery to them. For instance, they didn't know germs existed, so they mostly believed it was smells that made people sick.

Electricity had been discovered in lightning, but no-one knew how to make it or use it, so there were no phones, televisions, or computers. There were no cars, trains, or planes to travel in, so it was much harder to get around, and plastic hadn't even been invented.

People didn't have the same chances we do to find out about what has happened in the world either, or learn from it, so most people had no idea about the importance of taking care of the world or of treating people fairly.

Our story starts in town called Waterside, which was a seaside town with a harbour. The Harbourmaster was Bill, who lived there with his wife Mary, and their adopted daughter Clara, who had just turned twenty-one. With the help of Clara, Mary ran a class three mornings a week, to teach children to read and write. In those days there were no schools for everyone, so it was the only chance for most children to learn, unless their parents taught them.

Bill had lived in Waterside Harbour all his life and had grown up with Clara's father, Cyrus Yonder. Cyrus had gone to sea and eventually become a pirate captain. He'd brought Clara, his only child, to live with Bill and Mary when she was 5 years old.

Bill ran a strict harbour and pirate ships were not allowed to dock there, but everyone knew there was a small deep cove just along the coast, where pirate ships often dropped anchor for rest and repair. Bill was a fair man and had made an agreement with the town's Mayor that, as long as the pirates didn't attack any ships in the area, and were well behaved when they came into town, then they would be treated the same as everyone else.

Waterside Harbour was not a rich place, and there were plenty of poor families, but because so many ships came there it was thriving. The ships brought people from all over the world, it didn't matter if they were sailors, merchants, or pirates as long as they came and ate, drank, and spent money in the shops there ... some of them had even stayed and had families who lived in the town.

In recent years Clara's birth father, Cyrus, who as a pirate was known to everyone just as Captain C, had come back to find her and stayed, tired of the pirating life. Although she hadn't seen him since she was eight, she had forgiven him for leaving her. She understood why he had not been able to come back, and Bill and Mary had been good loving parents to her... they had given her a love for life, the land, and the sea. She had also always enjoyed meeting the different kinds of people who came to Waterside and loved hearing about the world. Now she loved to listen to the stories her father told her about the things he had seen, and the life he had lived, even though much of it had not been happy or good.

Clara worked in both a local shop (in the afternoons) and a local pub (in the evenings), to save money for her future; she didn't plan to stay in Waterside all her life. She'd heard about the world out there; how beautiful and varied it was, and some of the happy and sad things happening in it. Her dream was to go out there, see as much of the world as possible, and do what she could to make it a happier place.

The pub she worked in was where you could usually find Captain C. He wanted to be near her and hear about her hopes and dreams. He hoped that one day, he might be able to help them come true, as he deeply regretted that he had not made a better use of his life.

One evening in the pub, a man Clara had not seen before came asking for Captain C. He looked like a pirate and was not much younger than her father. Captain C greeted him like a long-lost friend but didn't bring him over and introduce him to Clara.

Clara tried to keep an eye on them, hoping for a chance to go over and find out who the man was, but it was a busy night, and the opportunity didn't arise. They seemed deep in discussion. Towards closing time, when it was most busy, Clara lost track of them and the next time she looked, her father and the strange man were gone; they'd slipped out without her even noticing.

The next morning as Bill, Mary and Clara were enjoying a hearty breakfast of bacon and eggs, there was a knock at the door. It was her father wanting to speak to them. They rustled up some more food for him and, as they ate together, he told them about the strange man Clara had seen the night before.

It turned out that he was one of her father's old pirate crew; the one who had taken over as Captain when he left. Apparently, they had got hold of a new ship which was much quicker and in better condition, and they were asking Captain C whether he would like the old one, as it had been his ship for so many years. The ship was anchored in the pirate cove, and Captain C had been to see it when he had left the pub the previous evening.

Clara felt a surge of excitement. Something inside her told her this might be the opportunity she had been waiting for, a chance to do something she had aspired to do for a long time. She took a deep breath and told them her idea.

Her father, Bill and Mary were all aware of her dream, so they weren't surprised about the suggestion she made to them. They talked together for a long time about what could be done with the ship and eventually they had a plan. Bill agreed the ship could be brought into the harbour as it needed repair, but Clara and Captain C asked if their actual plan could remain a secret for a little longer.

Chapter 2: The Mystery Ship

Two days later everyone in Waterside woke to find a strange ship in the harbour; moored in the place where ships were put to make repairs. It must have arrived overnight, but no-one had seen it come. There was nothing very unusual about that, but there were two things about this ship that were odd.

Firstly, it had the look of a pirate ship, and everyone knew that pirate ships were not allowed in the harbour, so what was it doing there?

Secondly, it was a mystery ship. It had no name that anyone could see, and no crew seemed to have arrived with the ship. In fact, as far as anyone could find out no-one seemed to know how it got there, where it had come from, or who it belonged to.

By lunchtime that day everyone in the town was talking about it and trying to solve the mystery.

Phoebe, a young girl in the town who made it her business to talk to everyone, was particularly keen to work out what was going on. When she found no-one could tell her anything useful, she decided the Harbourmaster must be the one who would know, so she headed down to the harbour that evening to ask. As she approached, she saw the Harbourmaster, Captain C and Clara coming off the ship, and then standing on the pier next to it pointing and talking. Clara appeared to be taking notes.

Phoebe wasn't rude, so she didn't want to interrupt them and hung back at a distance until they were finished. When Captain C and the Harbourmaster left, Clara stayed and stood there for a while longer just looking at the ship. It was obvious Clara knew at least something about it.

Phoebe saw her opportunity. She considered Clara her friend, so it seemed natural to ask her what was going on.

"Hi Clara," she said, "interesting ship… do you know who it belongs to?"

"Err, yes," said Clara, putting her notes behind her back; she knew how much Phoebe liked talking to everyone. "… but the Harbourmaster has been asked not to tell everyone yet," she continued, "so I can't tell you. It is a lovely ship though don't you think?"

"I suppose so," said Phoebe, rather puzzled by this, as to her it actually looked rather old and tatty. "It needs a bit of cleaning up though doesn't it, and it doesn't seem to have a name!"

"No, not yet" said Clara, smiling rather more than normal, "… and yes, it does need some work and a clean-up, but it's not in bad condition for an old ship. The owner is looking for people to help get it ship-shape and then maybe even crew it… if they're the right people."

"What sort of ship is it going to be?" asked Phoebe, "It looks like a pirate ship, but we all know the Harbourmaster wouldn't let a pirate ship in here!"

"Maybe he would … if it was a Positive Pirate ship." said Clara, sounding strangely pleased with the idea. Phoebe thought she was behaving rather oddly.

"What on earth is a Positive Pirate?" asked Phoebe.

"Good question" Clara replied, still being rather mysterious. "I can't say now, but I suppose people will need to be told, so they can decide if this is an opportunity for them. What do you think's the best way to do that?"

"Well, it all sounds very mysterious to me" said Phoebe, wondering how she was supposed to advise Clara about something when she herself had no idea what she was talking about! "… but I suppose nothing gets people more interested than a mystery. So, maybe you could just tell people a time when someone is going to solve the mystery, and maybe they would come to find out."

"Hmm," said Clara thoughtfully, looking back at the ship as if it was going to tell her the answer.

Phoebe thought of something else she wanted to ask.

"You mentioned 'The right sort of people'... who are the right sort of people?"

"Oh. Yes" said Clara, looking back at Phoebe, "I think the right sort of people will ... be excited by the idea of an adventure and the chance to become part of the crew when the ship is ready." It wasn't really the answer Phoebe was hoping for, so she pressed on.

"Does that mean they only want people who have already been sailors ... and err, only boys or men?" asked Phoebe suspiciously; she liked a mystery more than most, and certainly liked the idea of an adventure, so, she'd started to hope she might be the right kind of person, whatever that was, and she certainly didn't want to be left out.

"Oh no... anyone can join!" said Clara, but then quickly added ... "as far as I understand. As long as there are a few people who know about ships and the others are willing to learn. You're right, people will need to be invited somewhere to hear about the opportunity."

"Okay" said Phoebe, secretly relieved. "Well, the grass over there by the harbour would be a good place to ask people to come. It's right near the shops, so if people see a crowd gathering, they might just join in, and you can see the ship from there. When is this going to happen?"

"Oh ... I'm not sure yet," said Clara, then added quickly, "I need to check." She suddenly felt this was all happening too fast. "Can we talk about it tomorrow morning; if you're happy to help with getting people to come?"

"Yes of course!" said Phoebe, laughing, "I want the mystery solved as much as anyone!"

They agreed to meet up bright and early the next morning, then went their separate ways. Phoebe walked home, wondering about the mystery of Positive Pirates and who the Captain was going be; and Clara went to the pub where she was working that evening, thinking about the next step in the plan.

Later, when the pub was closing, Clara asked her father to stay and walk with her. They walked down by the harbour. It was one of Clara's favourite places, with the slush, slush of the waves in the background, and the clanging sound of the wind in the masts of the ships, it made her feel at home. She told him what had happened with Phoebe, and how eager she'd said people were to solve the mystery of the ship. He sensed she was reluctant in some way.

"That sounds like good news to me!" he said. "You can't hide a ship from people for long once it's in the harbour, so they were bound to ask questions. It is a good thing people are interested, isn't it?"

"Well yes, I suppose so," said Clara hesitantly, "it just feels very fast." She took a deep breath and then puffed it out loudly; the decision made. "It seems it's time to tell people about Positive Pirates. Part of me just can't believe this is actually happening after all this time! I guess I'm nervous."

"Of course," said her father kindly, "that's only natural. Let's go and tell Bill and Mary." Then he smiled, kissed her forehead affectionately, and they walked home together, so they could break the news and talk through the details of how it could all work.

Chapter 3: Spreading the Word

True to her word Phoebe was there the next morning. She'd been thinking about the mystery ship overnight. She felt sure the Captain was Captain C, Clara's real father, and that was why Clara was so involved, but she really wanted to know.

"Did you check with... er ... who was it again?" she asked, trying to trick Clara into telling her.

"I didn't say – but yes, it's all agreed." said Clara decisively. "It's been decided that we will get people here tomorrow morning and tell them about it being a Positive Pirate ship and what that means ... but I can't tell you any more until tomorrow."

"Oh, that's okay" said Phoebe, "I can wait till tomorrow. Do you want me to spread the word around?"

"Yes please, I get the feeling you would be good at that." said Clara. Phoebe smiled proudly, then she shared her plan.

"I'll tell everyone I have really exciting news," she said confidently, "that I hear there's going to be a big announcement about what they ship is for. I for one can't wait!"

They agreed a time for people to come the next morning, and both set off to spread the word. Clara had to go and help Mary with the class for reading and writing first, as she usually did, and as she walked there a thought struck her and she smiled to herself; someone at the class had come to mind, someone who she thought, and hoped, might be interested in the news too.

Phoebe set off to tell as many people as she could – especially the ones who she knew were good at spreading news fast, or gossiping, as some people would describe it. She'd lived here all her life, and paid attention to what different people were good at, so she knew exactly who to go to for this particular job.

A little later Phoebe was walking purposefully past the Tide's Inn, the pub where Clara worked in the evenings, when she came across her friend Solomon who was the son of the landlord. It was a warm day and he worked in the kitchen, so had come out to get some fresh air and a bit of a break. As he stood there, he'd noticed her going in and out of different buildings and talking very enthusiastically to everyone she met in the street.

"You seem busy Phoebe," he said, "what are you up to?"

Phoebe hadn't considered telling Solomon because she knew he'd been at sea before, and he'd had to come home when he injured his leg badly and ended up with a peg leg. Most ships wouldn't take someone with a peg leg, and even if they did, they'd mostly just make them work in the kitchen, or the galley as it's known on a ship. Phoebe had assumed that Solomon wouldn't be interested in that, although he obviously liked cooking as since he'd been home, he'd made a bit of a name for himself as a good cook at the pub.

Taking all that into account she wasn't sure if he would consider going back to sea, but as he had asked, she told him about the ship and what Clara had said about Positive Pirates.

"That sounds intriguing" he said, "but what exactly is a Positive Pirate ... and will they take people with peg legs?"

"To be honest I don't know" said Phoebe, "It's all rather mysterious. I can't even find out who owns the ship, but I have a fairly good idea it is Captain C. I think that's why Clara is so involved."

"Interesting" said Solomon, "I saw Clara talking to him when they left the pub last night so you might be right, but I thought he'd had enough of being at sea. What a puzzle. So, how do we find out more?"

"There's a meeting tomorrow where, from what I hear, all will be revealed!" said Phoebe grandly.

"Maybe I'll take my friend Ashar along too," Solomon said thoughtfully. "We like a puzzle, so I'm sure he'll be keen to find out what it's all about as well."

Phoebe told him the meeting time and place and he promised not only to tell Ashar, but to spread the word around to others in the pub as well.

Meanwhile Clara had talked to Dante, at the class. He was in his late teens and had only recently come to Waterside. He had asked to come to the lessons because he said he'd always had trouble learning to read and write; and it was true, he clearly struggled to learn. Clara wished she were a better teacher. However, he certainly wasn't stupid, and she could see he was kind, and a hard worker who obviously didn't give up easily, and that was just the sort of person she thought was needed. Dante agreed to come along, as it sounded like there might be an opportunity for something interesting.

Phoebe worked hard for the rest of the day getting the word out. By the time it was starting to get dark, she was exhausted and decided she'd done enough for the day. She was just taking a pleasant walk back home past the old church, listening to the sound of the birds starting to roost in the trees, when she came across Alik. He was the oldest son in a large family who lived up at the other end of the road from her, next to the woods. He was just walking back home after dropping some vegetables into her parent's shop. She decided maybe she had the energy to tell one more person. He sounded quite interested in her story.

"I might just go along" he said, "it'll be interesting to hear what Positive Pirates are... I've certainly never heard of them, but I like the idea of a positive team and an adventure!"

Chapter 4: The Invitation

The next morning there was quite a crowd of people at the appointed place near the harbour. You could hear the murmur of them talking before you could see them, so the noise definitely attracted some more people. As Phoebe had anticipated, they had mostly come to find out what was going on with the ship and who the Captain was going to be – even though Clara had said nothing about the Captain being revealed. When Bill, the Harbourmaster, arrived with Clara, it went quiet.

"So ... what's the big mystery and who is the Captain of this ship?" called out one brave person.

"Looks like a pirate ship to me" said another, "what's it doing in our harbour?"

"I'm not able to tell you who the Captain is at the moment," said Bill. "I have allowed it into our harbour because I am assured that, whilst it has been used as a pirate ship before, it will no longer be used for piracy."

"How can we be sure about that?" came the reply and there were murmurs of agreement.

"Because I know what it will be used for" said Bill in a no-nonsense way, "and, if you give us a chance, we will tell you more about that in a moment." He waited for the murmurs to die down before continuing.

"As you can see it is an old ship, and it needs cleaning up. We've been given the job of getting a team together to help with that. Firstly, Clara is going to explain a bit more about what the Captain plans to use the ship for. Hopefully, this will help you understand why you don't need to worry about its pirate background."

Clara stepped forward and took a deep breath.

"This ship" she said in her biggest, loudest voice, "is going to be used as a Positive Pirate ship.

"What on earth does that mean?" shouted a loud, and not very friendly voice from near the back.

Clara remembered to stay calm, took another deep breath, and carried on.

"If you give me time, I will tell you." she said assertively, "... as we all know, there are actually some good things about pirates. Firstly, they are good at working in a team..."

"That's true" interrupted a voice from the crowd "there've been many sailors who have abandoned ship to be pirates, because pirates treat each other as equals!"

"Yes," said another voice from a group that looked like they might be pirates, "... and it's well known they share their treasure between them."

There was a murmur of approval and looking around she could see several people nodding, especially the group that looked like they were pirates ... but she didn't allow herself to be put off.

"Yes" she said quickly "they are well known for working as a team and sharing their treasure with each other.... however, they think 'treasures' are things that belong to other people, so they steal them, then hide them away to stop others from getting them. So, what they do makes other people unhappy and afraid. They do it because they believe there is never enough to go around, so they think they need to take & keep things for themselves."

... a murmur spread around the crowd, Clara couldn't quite tell if they were agreeing with her or not. Certainly, the pirates were not looking that happy at being described this way, but she knew what she had said was true, so she pressed on...

"Positive Pirates are also good at working in a team and they will share their treasures with each other as well. The difference is that they realise that the real treasures are things they already have, or can learn, not things they have to steal from others. Positive Pirates not only share their treasure with each other, they go out and share what they have with anyone. They use their treasures to help others and make the world a better and happier place; because they know that when they share, then there is plenty for everyone."

There was silence when she finished. People looked at each other and tried to take in what she had said. After what seemed to Clara like an awfully long time (but was really only a few seconds) Phoebe started clapping and it didn't take long till most of the crowd joined her. Clara felt very relieved.

There were a few people who started to wander off at this point as it wasn't for them, but Clara had expected that to happen. She knew the message would not please everyone. Right at that moment she was just very relieved to have got it out. She was so distracted by what was happening, that, for a moment, she completely forgot what she was going to say next ... but after a short silence, she took another deep breath and quickly remembered.

"This ship will be a Positive Pirate ship and the Captain wants you to know that if you are willing to come and join in, and bring your treasure, then anyone is welcome, whether you have been at sea before or not, as long as you are willing to learn! Having said that, of course, having some people who have been at sea would be very useful!"

"What kind of treasure are you talking about?" asked someone from the pirate group.

"Will we get paid?" asked another. Clara decided to answer the first question first.

"The treasure the Captain is asking you to bring, are the things you are good at, and the strengths you have; although I'm sure the Captain will consider anything you have to offer."

"Do you need fruit and vegetables?" asked Alik, "we have some spare; they could feed the crew."

"Oh ... yes ... that's very kind," said Clara. She was worried for a moment that people had missed the point and were still thinking the treasure she wanted was 'things'. She knew she needed to bring them back to her main point, without sounding rude about what they were offering.

"Anything you have to offer is appreciated," she continued, "but food will be provided for the workers. As I said, it is your strengths and skills we are really looking for; those are the treasures we on the hunt for, rather than money or the practical things you can bring!"

"So... will we get paid?" the same voice came again, sounding impatient. Clara took a deep breath.

"The Captain knows that you will need some time to decide if this is for you... and we need workers to sort out the ship – so, we have money to pay people for three days and we will also provide food. After that there will be no more pay, and you will need to decide if being a Positive Pirate is for you."

There was a murmur in the crowd and the group of pirates looked a little more interested.

"If you want to be a Positive Pirate" Clara continued, "then come along on the fourth day. You'll meet the Captain, and you will need to say what particular 'treasure' you will bring to the ship if you stay. You will need to say how that treasure has helped you... and how you think it can help others if you share it. Then the Captain will choose the crew."

"Will the crew get paid?" asked the same voice from the crowd.

"They won't be paid with money" said Clara, "but they won't go without food or somewhere to live."

"Huh ... it'll take a brave person to take up that offer!" said the voice dismissively.

"The three days start tomorrow morning, please come along here at 9am if you want to be involved," finished Clara positively, taking no notice of the voice.

With that said, many of the crowd left ... but there were quite a few who stayed, and they all started to talk amongst themselves. Even some of the pirates stayed talking to others who had remained behind.

Clara hoped as hard as she could, that enough people would turn up the next day, but most of all, that at least some of them would come on the fourth day as well.

Chapter 5: The Three Days

The next morning when Clara arrived at the ship, she was very relieved to find she was not alone; there were quite a few people there, including Phoebe. Some seemed to have brought things with them, one of them was Alik, who stepped forward immediately with a box of fruit and vegetables.

"I've brought these to help feed people," he said enthusiastically, "they're from our garden."

"Thank you," said Clara, a little worried it was the only reason he was there, "that is kind, but are you staying too?"

"Yes, definitely," he said, "being a Positive Pirate sounds just what I have been looking out for."

"Oh, that's wonderful," beamed Clara, "have the rest of you all come to be Positive Pirates too?"

Before anyone could answer, a small, but noisy group arrived, who were clearly from the pirate cove.

"We're not interested in being part of the crew, but you need hands on deck to mend the ship, and we could do with the money, so we're all willing to stay for as long as we get paid!" explained one of the pirates whose name was Rocco. He was a young but very large, dark-skinned man with braided hair and scars on his arms.

"Oh," said Clara, a little disappointed. "Thank you, that will help, but as I said, it will only be for three days." Then she turned to the rest of the crowd and asked again how many of them had come to be Positive Pirates.

A few people came forward saying that they were sorry, they couldn't get away to be Positive Pirates right now, but they loved the idea so had brought things they hoped would help instead. Clara had tears in her eyes when she saw how generous people had been. They piled the things up on the deck of the ship – it included:

- Quite a lot of wood and some rope
- Tools that they could use to do the mending (hammers, nails, saws, needles, thread)
- Paint & polish (along with brushes)
- More food
- Material for sails
- Buckets, mops, and cleaning rags

Whilst the people who had brought stuff were piling it up, under the supervision of Phoebe and Alik who had volunteered without being asked, Solomon came up to Clara and took her to one side.

"I need to ask you something" he said mysteriously,

"Go ahead" said Clara happily, she knew Solomon from the pub and was pleased to see him there.

"Well, you know very well that I have a peg leg" he said, without waiting for an answer, "so I need to know whether the captain will think that's a reason not to take me on. Will it mean I can't be part of the crew... do you know?"

"Are you willing to be a crew member with a peg leg?" asked Clara. "To be honest, I'm not sure what effect it will have on what you can do, but you presumably have an idea."

"I can do most things if I put my mind to it," said Solomon confidently, "but I don't think I'd be particularly good at climbing the rigging without a lot of practice. I'm willing to give anything a try!"

"Then if I know anything, I'm sure the Captain will be willing, or even proud, to have you as part of the crew" said Clara confidently. "Although of course you will have to convince the captain by saying what treasure you are planning to bring, like everyone else. Is that acceptable to you as an answer?"

"Indeed, it is!" said Solomon happily, and he walked back to tell his friend Ashar, who had been watching from a distance with a slightly concerned look on his face.

Once all the gifts that had been brought had been collected, and those who couldn't stay had left, the gang was much smaller, but there were at least twenty people left of all ages, types, and sizes. This included Rocco and a small group of pirates, and Clara was pleased to see it also included not only Phoebe and Solomon but Dante, Ashar and Alik as well.

They went onto the ship and walked around. At first glance it was obvious that there was quite a bit of cleaning, painting, and polishing that needed doing, along with some minor repairs. Those who were more familiar with ships, could also see the tell-tale signs that there may be some slightly bigger tasks that needed to be done before the ship would be properly sea-worthy, but it was Clara who spoke first.

"The Captain is aware there are some bigger jobs to do before we set sail," she said confidently, "but has asked that at the moment we focus on the more minor repairs and cleaning it up. This will give you a chance to work together and get to know the ship, before deciding whether you are interested in joining the crew. Once the crew is selected, we'll focus on the other work that needs to be done."

Rocco and the pirates seemed to think they would be in charge, but Clara made it clear that everyone would have a say in what needed doing and who would do what.

Phoebe suggested it would be useful to know what skills they each had, to help them decide who did what jobs, so they all went around and said whether they had worked on a ship before and what practical skills they had that might help.

Solomon reasoned that those who had experience with ships should go around and make a list of all the things they could see needed to be done, so that Clara could check with the Captain which jobs they were to focus on. Alik, who admitted he had not sailed a ship before, offered to work with the others to organise any cleaning and painting that clearly needed doing.

Once the list of jobs was agreed they made another list of other materials they needed to get. Clara said there was enough money and Phoebe offered to go into the town to get them, as she knew the best places to buy things cheaply. Ashar and one of the pirates went to help bring stuff back.

Once they had what they needed, jobs were allocated. They seemed to be working well as a team until Rocco, who was very full of himself and keen to be in charge, decided that everyone should have written instructions. Clara noticed that several people looked rather uncomfortable at this idea, but Rocco didn't notice, and was about to set off to write them. She decided to wait and see if anyone else in the team would say anything. It was Dante, the smallest one there, who spoke up.

"Actually Rocco, that won't work for me, as I can't read well," he said bravely.

"Ah, not clever enough, eh?" said Rocco unkindly, smirking at his other pirate friends.

"I didn't say I'm not clever," replied Dante assertively, "just that I've never learned to read well."

Rocco looked rather surprised at someone standing up to him, especially this small rather pale looking lad. He looked at his pirate buddies for support, but several of them looked away so he couldn't catch their eyes. Alik and Ashar noticed this too and suspected it was because they couldn't read either.

"I am sure he isn't the only one who can't read," said Alik, who was impressed by the fact that Dante had been prepared to stand up to Rocco, who was quite big and scary looking. "It's not that unusual after all! So, it's a kind offer, but we don't really need written instructions thank you."

"In fact, drawings might work better anyway," added Ashar quickly, "I've noticed before, that it's easier to see which bit of a ship is being referred to with a drawing, it avoids confusion."

"... I'm not doing drawings!" exclaimed Rocco roughly.

"You're just saying that because you can't draw!" said one of the other pirates called Frank, a small bloke with long black braided hair tied messily at the back of his head with a dirty bandana. Rocco turned on him angrily, as if he was about to punch him.

"I could help. I'm quite good at drawings," offered Dante quickly, "but I don't know the workings of ships as well as you do Rocco, and I can't spell. Maybe we could work together; you tell me the different parts of the ship where work needs doing, I'll make drawings and you can label them with instructions."

"Oh... okay." said Rocco, secretly relieved that had got sorted. He didn't like Frank, who could never keep his big mouth shut, but he didn't want to show himself up by getting into a fight over it.

After that, the team worked very well and Clara even noticed that Rocco and Dante went off together that evening; they looked almost comical, huge dark Rocco with small pale Dante, seeming the best of friends. She wondered about Frank; there was something not quite right about him, but she couldn't work out what it was. He didn't seem to get on with the other pirates, and he certainly seemed to have a knack for upsetting people; Clara wondered what she would do if he wanted to be a Positive Pirate.

By the end of the three days the ship was in reasonable shape. No-one dared to ask who was going to turn up the next morning to meet the Captain and tell their stories to become a Positive Pirate, so they just said goodbye, like they had every other night, when they went home at the end of the day.

Chapter 6: The Captain Revealed

Positive Pirate selection day was a sunny one with a beautiful blue sky, which seemed very fitting to Clara. Her father had come early to have breakfast with her, Bill, and Mary, although Clara was so nervous, she hardly ate anything. With breakfast over, she was keen to set out, even though it took no time at all to get to where everyone had been told to come, which was the same place as a few days previously. Consequently, they got there quite a long time before any of the potential Positive Pirates were due to arrive.

The others stayed on the grass waiting, but Clara wanted to collect her thoughts, so she went and stood at the end of the harbour wall for a while by herself. With the wind in her face, and the smell of the sea all around, it didn't take long before she felt calmer and ready for whatever the day would bring.

As the meeting time approached, Clara still found herself feeling nervous again and secretly a little bit worried that no-one would turn up, but she really believed in the idea, so she held on tight to that, and told herself they could make it happen somehow.

Then, right on time, a few people started to arrive. Phoebe came first; then Solomon and Ashar together, carrying a large box between them; then Alik; then Dante and finally, to Clara's surprise, Rocco wandered up, looking slightly sheepish. No sign of Frank or the others pirates though.

"Welcome everyone," said Clara, "I had hoped there might be a few more, but we are extremely glad to see you all here."

"Eerrm … I'm not here to be a Positive Pirate," said Rocco looking awkward. "I do like the idea, but I don't have a treasure and I need to send money to help my family, so I'm still needing the usual kind of treasure! I haven't got any other way to help them so I can't risk not having any. I came because I ... er... I ... just wanted to see who the Captain was."

"Oh, I see," said Clara, finding herself disappointed. "That's a shame, but I'm glad you like the idea."

"Talking to others around the town," added Phoebe, "I think a lot of people really like the idea but want to give other kinds of treasure to help, like the people who brought stuff on the first day."

"Yes," agreed Ashar, "and listening to others, some wanted to come but, like Rocco, they didn't know what treasure they had to offer ... a lot of people find it hard to say what they're good at."

"Those are good points," agreed Clara thoughtfully; she decided to let them continue.

"Maybe some people just aren't ready yet," added Dante, "they may still be developing their treasures, but might want to come another time."

"I think there might be quite a few other people, like Rocco," said Solomon, "who can't just leave what they are doing and set sail to be a Positive Pirate right now. There may even be some who are ill or injured or have disabilities that mean they can't sail on a ship, but they might want to help in other ways too."

"Maybe," said Alik thoughtfully, "people need to have choices about different ways they can help with what the Positive Pirates are trying to achieve. There are lots of different ways people could help." Then he had another thought, "maybe some people could come as trainees, to learn what their treasures are, or just come for one voyage."

As Clara listened to all the ideas that were coming out, a smile spread across her face; she could tell already that this was going to be a good Positive Pirate team.

"You make some excellent points," said Clara. "Maybe the Captain would like to explore them with you when we have sorted out who the crew is, but I suspect we might want to do that first."

Rocco, however, had also been listening to what the others said, and wanted to make a suggestion.

24

"I might be up for coming on one voyage," he said slightly cautiously. "I'm not sure I want to be called a 'trainee', but after being in a team with you all this week I have realised that I do have some things to learn, and I would like to carry on and help to get you started. Would the Captain allow that?"

Rocco had turned to Captain C when he asked the question. He, like Phoebe, had assumed that Captain C was the mysterious Captain. Seeing Rocco had made the same assumption as her, Phoebe was so pleased that she had worked this out too, that she couldn't contain herself any longer.

"Yes..." she said excitedly, looking at Captain C "... it *is* you, isn't it?"

Captain C looked a bit taken aback. He didn't respond straight away but looked at Clara.

"I think you might be barking up the wrong tree there," interrupted Solomon, "just because he *was* a Captain doesn't mean he *is* the Captain here!"

"That's true," added Ashar, "haven't you noticed who is the one really fired up by the idea of Positive Pirates ... and who has been taking charge round here?"

There was silence for a moment ... then all eyes turned to Clara. She smiled again.

"Yes, it's me!" she said proudly, very happy she didn't have to keep the secret any longer.

"Brilliant!" shouted Phoebe, who could have been upset at being wrong, but who was really rather pleased at this turn of events.

Rocco looked shocked for a minute, but then nodded acceptingly, smiled, and very deliberately looked at Clara when he said, "What do you think then Captain? – I told you I had a lot to learn!"

"I think it's a great idea Rocco." said Clara, then she thought for a moment before continuing. "Maybe rather than call you a trainee we could have a fun way to show the difference between committed Positive Pirates and other crew members. How about, when Positive Pirates join the crew, they get a nickname starting with P. ... so that they're all PPP (Positive Pirate P...)? You could use them as much or as little as you like, but anyone who isn't a full crew member wouldn't have one."

Everyone thought that was worth giving a try, but before they started, Captain C wanted to speak.

"Just to be clear," said Captain C, "Bill, Mary and I are here because we love Clara, and we want to support her dream and hear about her new team ... this is all Clara's idea... she has always wanted to see the world and make things in it better, and we are immensely proud of her."

"Thank you." Clara said, smiling at her family, then she turned to the others.

"Right, let's get on with the selection of the Positive Pirates! I don't think there is much question in my mind that you will all be chosen, I know you probably all have many treasures to bring, but I want to hear about the one that is most important to you. I'm really looking forward to hearing the stories of your treasures and how you think they can help, and when each of you is finished you can tell me the Positive Pirate nickname you'd like to have."

Chapter 7: Alik's Treasure

They all agreed they would like to hear each other's stories and Alik chose to go first – which he felt was exactly right, given what treasure he was bringing.

"The treasure I am bringing is being Responsible," Alik started proudly. "To me this means that I think about the consequences of what I do, and I do my best to make choices that lead to good consequences for myself, those around me ... and the world."

"That sounds great," said Clara, "Tell us about how this has helped you and how it will help others when you use it as a Positive Pirate." Alik nodded happily and continued.

"Being Responsible has helped me in three ways and they are all to do with my family. I am the oldest of seven children and life growing up was tough as we didn't have much money; my dad was always away at sea, and my grandad was often ill and needed looking after. It was my grandad who helped me to understand what being responsible meant, and this is what I've learned, and how it's helped me:

"Thinking about the choices I am making, and what effect they are having on my life:

"For some time, I didn't realise that by choosing not to help my mum, I was making my own life more difficult as well as hers. I thought that because I was a child, and she was our mum, she was supposed to do everything for everyone ... and be kind and loving all the time as well.

"When she expected things from me, or I didn't think she was being kind and loving, I got cross with her and blamed her for making me feel grumpy. All I thought about was how unfair it was that she was making my life hard. In fact, she was miserable and grumpy because she was so busy and tired and never got any help;

she wasn't trying to make my life hard; she was struggling with her own hard life.

"After a particularly bad day, when I was very rude to her, my grandad helped me see that the choices I was making, not to help or do things for myself, were not only making my mum's life harder; they were making my own life more miserable too. I was making things worse, not better.

"I realised that if I made different choices, things could be different. I could do some things for myself... and even help her.

"When I tried making different choices by helping, I found I actually felt much better about myself, and that made me happier. My different choices also meant she was less miserable and grumpy with me, so life got better in lots of ways ... it didn't take away the fact that we were poor, but it made being poor nowhere near as unpleasant.

"Understanding how much what I choose affects others as well as me:

"Once I understood that my choices had a big effect on my own life, as well as my mum's, I also started to realise that my choices were influencing my brothers too: they were copying me by being unhelpful. Some of them were still young and small, but others, like me, were old enough to help more.

"Unfortunately, they didn't really notice that I was being more helpful, as it didn't make much difference to them. Then, when I chose to try and tell them to be more helpful, they didn't think I had the right to tell them what to do and just got cross with me.

"Eventually, rather than choosing to try to boss them around, I chose to tell them what I had realised about my own behaviour and admit the ways I had made things worse for everyone. It was a much better choice as, rather than being cross about being bossed around, they started to think about what they were doing too, and they made some changes for themselves.

"Finding out that when people make good choices as a team, they can make a big difference:

"Us older ones had happy memories of playing in the garden when we were younger; as the oldest, when I was young, I'd spent many happy hours with my grandad there growing fruit and vegetables.

"Unfortunately, as we grew up, he became ill, and it wasn't long before he was so old and sick that he couldn't even get outside. The garden became a mess, a dumping ground we avoided.

"When I was thirteen, I decided to try and sort the garden out by myself. Unsurprisingly, it became obvious pretty quickly that I wouldn't get far doing it alone, and I had to accept I needed help.

"To cut a long story short, we decided to work together as a team. We all had different ideas and skills to bring to the job, and it took a while to learn how to work as a team, but in the end, it turned out even better than I had imagined.

"We made a place to grow fruit and vegetables, some space for our smaller brothers and sister to play, and even somewhere for Grandad to sit outside so he could join in. Everyone was much happier. We had learned that a few people being responsible together in a team, can make a big difference, and succeed where one person by themselves may not be able to."

"Yes!" said Clara, "you brought us some of those fruits and vegetables on the first day! I can see now why you were so proud to bring them. Tell us how you think being Responsible can be a treasure Positive Pirates can share."

"Okay," said Alik. "I think being responsible will help us on the ship – when we're a team together. We've already been doing this when we were cleaning the ship up.

"We needed to be responsible, and aware, about how our choices were affecting each other … like Rocco needing to realise that writing instructions didn't work for everyone. As a team we all made choices to face the problem and share ideas so that we found a better way of working.

"I'm sure that wherever we go and try to make things better, it will often mean helping people look at their choices. Helping them to see whether the consequences they are causing are really what they want, whether they are making life better or worse.

"Also, some changes need people to work in a team, and teams where everyone is being responsible, and playing their part, are much more successful."

"Thank you Alik," said Clara. "I am certainly convinced that your treasure of being Responsible is a very valuable one. I would very much like you to join us and be a Positive Pirate, and part of our team. Have you thought about what nickname beginning with P you would like?"

"Yes" said Alik, "I would like to be known as Patch please. It was my grandad's nickname for me when I was little, and I used to help him with his vegetable patch. It seems right since it was my Grandad who helped me understand how being Responsible could make my life better."

"Welcome Alik, or Positive Pirate Patch" said Clara, "our first ever Positive Pirate!"

Everyone clapped.

Chapter 8: Dante's Treasure

Dante said he would like to go next.

"The treasure I want to bring to share is Resilience. Resilience is the ability to stick at things and not give up. To me that means being able to find good in even the most difficult situations, so that you can keep going and bounce back when things are hard or don't go the way you want."

"That sounds like quite a treasure Dante," smiled Clara, "and I have already seen it in you. We'd love to hear more about how you became resilient, how it has helped you, and why you think it is an important thing for us to share as Positive Pirates."

"A lot of things have happened in my life that have helped me become Resilient," said Dante. "Maybe it would help to start by telling you a tiny bit about where I come from."

"When I was a baby, we lived in a country that had suffered a lot from wars and we were extremely poor. My parents were afraid for us, and although my dad couldn't leave, he eventually persuaded my mum, granny, and grandpa to leave with me and my brother, who was seven at the time. We ended up in a town called Lowestoft, which is where I grew up. This is what I've learned about being resilient:

"Being resilient means choosing how you look at things, even in the saddest or hardest times:

"I don't remember my dad as I was too little when we left, and I never saw him again. My mum was always sad, but she worked extremely hard, along with my grandpa, to make money and provide food for us all.

"As she was so busy, I didn't see my mum as much as I would have liked, but it meant that I spent most of my time with my granny, who I called my Babula, and looking back, that was a real treasure.

31

"She helped me to understand that what dad had done was because he loved us all, and what my mum was doing now (working so hard) was for the same reason. She helped me see I was incredibly lucky to have had such loving parents.

"I realise now that she taught me that I can choose how to look at things. She helped me discover that if I look carefully, I can find, or make, good things out of every situation, was the start of learning to be resilient.

"She used to say, 'every cloud has a silver lining... you just need the right glasses to see it!'

"She always helped me see the silver lining, and it was from her I learned that I need to change my glasses sometimes to help me see things differently!

"Being resilient means sticking at things, even when they are difficult:

"We were lucky because there was a school in Lowestoft, but I always had trouble learning to read and write... the letters always just seemed to move about on the page.

"It started the same with numbers, but Babula (my granny) said I could do it if I kept trying, so I didn't give up. She helped me practice counting the apples and potatoes and the money she got from selling them – now I'm brilliant with numbers; I can even do complicated sums in my head.

"She told me that it's not only how I look at things that's important, what I tell myself about them is important too!

"She said don't look at things as impossible or tell myself I'll never be able to do them, or they will seem impossible.

"Also never look at myself, or describe myself, as a failure ... always tell myself 'I can' and that 'I'm just learning', then I just need to keep practicing, and stick at things till I get there. It works!

"Managing my emotions has helped me to get through things:

"It's a long story, but a while back, after my granny had left to live elsewhere, I decided that I was going to be a fisherman. I told myself I could do it if I wanted to, so I found a broken old boat and repaired it by myself, then I rowed out to sea one morning with my net.

"The trouble was I didn't know much about boats, but I didn't get help with repairing the boat and it sprung a leak and sank.

"I'm quite a good swimmer, but the current was very strong, and I'd gone too far from the shore; I knew I couldn't swim back so I started to panic. I thought I was going to drown. Then then I remembered what Babula had taught me about staying calm so you can think straight, and I tried it.

"I breathed slowly, and as I started to calm down, I remembered that floating on my back would save energy. Then I thought that if I put my scarf on the oar I'd managed to keep from the boat, and made it stick up like a flag, someone might see me.

"I'd floated there for hours before a pirate ship came past, but they saw my flag and picked me up.

"Noticing that I can bounce back from whatever happens, helps me know I am resilient:

"The pirate ship that picked me up wasn't willing to take me back to Lowestoft, so they dropped me off at their next stop ... which was the pirate cove near Waterside! Guess what – Waterside was where my granny was! We were so pleased to see each other.

"Looking back, I can see that each stage of my life where there were difficulties, and I could have just given up, I didn't.

"Sometimes I needed the help of others, but I always got through things. In fact, once I'd got past the hard bit, things ended up better than they were before. Realising that helped me to know I am resilient; if I can do it once, I can do it again ... any time.

"Weirdly, knowing I am resilient makes me even more resilient, because when I come across a new challenge, I know I have what is necessary to get through it, and make good come from it.

"It doesn't mean things aren't hard sometimes, and I may have difficult feelings to get past, but I know I can always bounce back!"

"Wow Dante," said Clara "I have a feeling that there is a much longer story you could tell us about your life, but you've certainly managed to bounce back from a lot of things. Tell us why you believe being Resilient is a treasure we should share as Positive Pirates."

"I came to Waterside well over a year ago," said Dante, "and now I'm ready for a new challenge. I want to be a Positive Pirate because we are going to try and make things better for people and the world.

"I know that when things need to be made better, it's because they are not good to start with. When things are not good, you need resilience to keep going and get to the place where they are good again, and that's why I think it's important.

"I may be small, but I'm brave, because I've learned that how you look at things, what you say to yourself about things, and knowing how to manage your emotions, are all important in turning bad things into good things, and that is what I want to help others to do."

"That is wonderful, Dante," said Clara. "We want you to do that too. Your treasure of being Resilient is an unbelievably valuable one and I would love you to join us and be a Positive Pirate. Have you thought about what nickname beginning with P you would like?"

"Brilliant," said Dante proudly. "Yes, I would like my positive pirate nickname to be Pavel, which means small.

"That name makes me smile inside because my brother used to call me that to tease me when I was little. Now it reminds me that even when you feel small, like I used to, and even look small on the outside, you can be big on the inside, and it is the inside that really matters."

"Welcome Dante, or Positive Pirate Pavel" said Clara, and everyone clapped; Rocco even cheered.

Chapter 9: Phoebe's Treasure

Phoebe was keen to be next. She started like the others had as it seemed to work well:

"The treasure I want to bring, and share is Resourcefulness. This means being good at finding ways to get what is needed in order to succeed at whatever it is you want to achieve."

"That does sound just like you and exactly the sort of thing we need as a team," said Clara. "Tell us some more about how being Resourceful has helped you and why you think it's an important thing for us to share as Positive Pirates."

"Unlike Alik and Dante, I haven't had a tough life," Phoebe started. "My parents ran a grocer's shop in Waterside, and as I was growing up it was going very well. I have a brother who is three years older than me and a sister two years younger, and whilst we weren't rich, we had everything we needed.

"Things changed when I was about twelve, just after my parents had borrowed money to buy and extend the house and shop.

"That year there were some terrible storms and there was a flood in our street. Water got into the shop and flooded everywhere, everything we had to sell was ruined. It's since then I have found that learning to be resourceful has really helped me, and my family. This is what I've learned:

"Being Resourceful means making sure you understand what is really needed:

"After the flood, my parents were in despair. They'd used all their money to buy and extend the shop, and they had nothing left to sell, and no money to buy more.

"What made it worse was that they'd borrowed money and they also needed to pay that back. They were convinced the way to solve the problem was to get more money from somewhere, even though that would put them into more debt. The trouble was no-one was willing to lend it to them.

"When we all asked questions about what we needed and why, we realised it wasn't money we needed to be asking for ... it was things to sell in the shop!

"We needed to take time to understand the real problem; having money could have been a solution, but there were other ways to solve the problem.

"Being resourceful means looking at the problem carefully so you can work out if there are different ways to solve it. We managed to solve it once we realised that.

"Being Resourceful means believing there is a way and deciding to find it:

"When my parents were just looking for money to solve the problem, they started to believe it wasn't possible. Feeling things were hopeless made them lose all their energy and they nearly gave up.

"I remembered what they'd always told us about believing in yourself as if we did that, we could do anything. I realised we needed to believe finding a solution was possible.

"Once we believed there must be a way to solve the problem, it gave us energy ... then we could use that energy to find what the solution was. It's exceedingly difficult to be creative and see possibilities when you feel hopeless.

"For us, deciding to believe it was possible to find a solution, and making the decision to find it, kept us going and helped us not to get put off when we didn't find the best way immediately.

"Believe there is a way, decide you can, and you will, even if it takes a while!

"Being Resourceful means knowing what you're good at and when you need help:

"Sometimes you can't succeed without the help of other people, so asking for help is a good thing.

"When we were trying to find things to sell in the shop, at first my parents were ashamed to tell people that we needed help. They wanted us to sort out the problem by ourselves.

"We knew we had a lot of good ideas and could see what was possible, but we soon realised that we needed other people to make our ideas work.

"My parents had always been kind and helped other people, so I was sure others would be willing to help us if we asked; and they were.

"Although my parents were shy about asking at first, when they saw how keen other people were to help us, and what a difference it made to what we could do, they were extremely happy.

"Even better, the solution ended up helping lots of people, not just us, so it was good for everyone, and we wouldn't have found it if we hadn't asked for help!

"Being Resourceful means getting to know others so you can help each other:

"As you know I have always liked talking to people and finding out about them and for me that's part of what makes me Resourceful.

"I've found when you take time to get to know people, and let them get to know you, you find ways that you can help each other. You find out what they are good at, what they know, and maybe also what they need help with.

"When I need help, I nearly always know the best person to go to, and they know they can come to me. It made my parents happy to be kind and helpful to people, and it makes me happy to do the same.

"Someone once told me kindness is like that – it makes you happy when you give it! But I've seen that it not only makes you happy, it seems that what you give, you also get back.

"People like to help people who have helped them, and when you have received kindness, you are more likely to give it.

"Sharing is a wonderful way to make sure everyone gets what they need."

"Thank you, Phoebe," said Clara. "I know some of us have already seen that what you've told us is true, as your resourcefulness means we already know you. I suspect you played a bigger part than you've let on in helping your own family, and I am sure they are very grateful. Tell us a bit about why you believe Being Resourceful is a treasure we should share as Positive Pirates."

"Well," continued Phoebe, "an important part of Being Resourceful is understanding where resources come from. I've found that some resources are things you have inside you, and you just need to find them and use them... but there are also lots of other resources that come from other places.

"Some of those resources are things you can find out about, and some are things that other people can bring. Without all these things working together, it's harder to be successful, or find the best solution.

"Our job will be to help people, and to do that we'll need to use all the resources in our team, but we'll need more than that. We'll also need to help other people realise they can be resourceful too.

"That will be especially important when we leave, because if they have learned to be resourceful then they will have learned how to solve things for themselves and with each other."

"That's very true," agreed Clara. "Being Resourceful is a lasting treasure, which is exactly what we want to give people.

"Also, I've already experienced how your resourcefulness can help us, as you knew all the right people to help spread the message about our opportunity in the first place! Most of the team are here because of you. Thank you, Phoebe."

Everyone burst into applause as they knew what Clara had said was true and they were only there because she had spread the word.

"So – welcome to the Positive Pirate team Phoebe." said Clara, "What would you like your Positive Pirate nickname to be?"

"Well," said Phoebe, "even though I already have a name that begins with P, I want to be the same as everyone else and chose another special name as my Pirate name. I chose Polly. I've always liked that name and it is easy for people to spell (which Phoebe isn't) and remember; it's good to be remembered."

"Welcome Phoebe, or Positive Pirate Polly" said Clara, and everyone clapped again.

Chapter 10: Solomon's Treasure

"**M**e next," said Solomon, "Ashar and I think our treasures go hand in hand, they kind of need each other, like we do, but we've agreed that I'll start.

"The treasure I want to bring, and share, is Reasoning.

"This means using your brain, your mind, to find and look at all the information and evidence available to you, and then to organise it so that you can learn from it and come to good conclusions.

"It's great for learning, solving problems and helping you to make good decisions."

"Good decisions and solving problems sound very useful," said Clara, "we'll look forward to hearing from Ashar after this but tell us more about what Reasoning means and how it's helped you."

"Okay," said Solomon, "here are some things I have learned about reasoning that have helped me:

"Reasoning means finding all the information, or evidence, you can, before making a decision:

"My mum used to call this 'playing detective' and the first time we all realised its importance was when some money went missing from the pub my parents run. It happened a few times before they realised it wasn't accidental.

"I overheard my parents talking about sacking one of the bar staff, Bob, for it. I liked Bob, so I asked what was going on.

"They told me it must be him as he was the only one who'd been working each time it had happened.

"That didn't make sense to me as I knew several of the other bar staff often came in on their nights off and went behind the bar.

"Also, it just so happened that I knew Bob wasn't short of money as he'd recently inherited some, so he had no need to steal.

"It turned out it wasn't Bob.

"My mum and dad had jumped to a conclusion on only one piece of evidence, and it was the wrong conclusion!

"It would have ended badly for Bob and us; we would have lost a good member of staff and still had the thief! Detectives never jump to conclusions!

"Reasoning involves sorting all the information out, to work out what it's telling you:

"The reason we realised it wasn't Bob was because we sorted out all the information we had.

"There were lots of different kinds of information, we needed to sort it out and work out what it was, and wasn't, telling us.

"Some kinds of information only give you clues, so they're not good to base decisions on by themselves. For example, the information about who was working each night was just a clue; it wasn't reliable because other staff still came in on their nights off and had the opportunity to steal.

"The information about who might need money was also a clue, but it wasn't reliable either because some staff might have needed money without us knowing.

"We also knew the people and Bob behaved like a very trustworthy character, but he might have been pretending so we wouldn't suspect him!

"None of those clues were enough by themselves, but when we put them all together, they suggested it wasn't Bob.

"When we looked at the patterns of who often came in on their night off, who had money troubles, and who seemed to be less reliable, there were a couple of other people it could have been.

"We realised we needed to gather more information, so we secretly watched the people we suspected every time they came in on a night off, and we caught one of them in the act.

41

"Reasoning uses questions to find things out, help think things through and explore ideas:

"I've always liked finding things out, and in the evenings, with my parents busy in the pub, I used to occupy myself by asking people questions.

"Questions are good for finding things out, but not everyone liked it, and one evening I asked a rather drunk bloke one too many questions and he asked me *"What if I box your ears – will that stop you asking stupid questions?"*

"My mum overheard and told him he would get kicked out of the pub, so he decided not to hit me, but it got me thinking that 'What if?" was a good question.

"The 'what if' question had helped us to think about the consequences of what we were doing, and that helped us both to make better decisions without anyone getting in trouble; he knew not to hit me, and I knew not to ask him any more questions!

"I found the 'What if ...' question was also really good at helping me think things through and explore ideas by myself. I asked myself, 'what if I never did my chores?' or 'what if I had run away and become a pirate?', or 'what if I snuck out this evening? ... you get the idea.

"Playing 'What If?' helped me imagine the outcome of different decisions without doing them, by using things I already knew to help me. It kept me out of a lot of trouble I can tell you!

"Sometimes I found someone willing to play 'What if?' with me. We'd imagine our way through lots of ideas like 'what if we ate as much as we wanted all the time?', it was fun, and I learned a lot.

"I still use it a lot; Ashar and I do it when trying to decide about things and I use it in the kitchen when I'm making up new recipes ... 'what if I add a bit of this?' Sometimes I try my idea out, but I often ask others first whether they've ever had that and if they think it would be nice – it helps me not to waste food by trying whacky ideas.

"It's important to realise things are not always what they seem:

"It's important to understand the difference between facts and opinions.

"My grandad was a notorious pirate from the Caribbean who was hanged for his crimes.

"He did terrible things as a pirate, but he was a good father when he was around: he played with his son, brought him gifts, and taught him to love the sea.

"My dad knew some of the bad things his dad had done as a pirate, but he didn't tell me. He only talked lovingly about him and shared his love of the sea with me too. So, I imagined that being a pirate was all wonderful; so much so, that when I was six, I packed my bags and told my dad I was off to be a pirate like my grandad.

"It was then he decided perhaps he needed to tell me some more of the story. He didn't mean to lie to me, but by only telling me some of the truth I got a false picture. He realised what he'd told me had given me a view of his dad that was a bit skewed… he was only telling me the dad bit, not the pirate bit.

"I was horrified to hear the truth at first but looking back I realise it was a good lesson…. Sometimes things are what they seem to be, but sometimes they aren't, especially when you don't know everything!

"Even people you trust can give you a false picture, accidentally, like my dad, or sometimes on purpose; they might be telling you their opinions, not facts, or they might want you to agree with them so much that they only tell you some of the facts and not all of them. That's where the other parts of reasoning are helpful as they can help you get more information and decide for yourself what the truth is.

"The other thing you need to bear in mind is that there's lots of stuff we just don't know all the facts about yet, so things are often a lot more complicated than we realise. So, when people say something is simple or that they know all there is to know about something they might well be wrong, even if they believe they are right.

"Always remember, if you can't be completely sure you have all the evidence, then find as much evidence as you can then go with that, but be aware, it's quite possible that things aren't what they seem to be!"

"That's really interesting Solomon," said Clara. "So now you're wanting to be a pirate again - but a positive one! I'm sure you have other interesting things you've worked out with your reasoning but tell us how you think this treasure will be useful for us to share as Positive Pirates."

"Sure," said Solomon. "I think we'll often need to help people solve problems that they might be struggling with, or to do things differently to help themselves or make things work better.

"Lots of people don't realise there's information and evidence that would help them, because they don't know how to look for it. It isn't just in books.

"Reasoning helps you to realise how important information and evidence is, but also helps you to use it and not get fooled by it so you don't jump to conclusions that are unhelpful or may even harm you."

"That sounds very important Solomon and I think you will be a very valuable addition to our team," said Clara. "Have you thought about what Pirate nickname you would like to have?"

"Sort of," said Solomon. "I had two ideas – I don't mind which, as I like them both ... you could choose which one you prefer – I was thinking of Percy or Pierre."

"Then welcome to the team Solomon, or Positive Pirate Percy!" and there was applause all round.

Chapter 11: Ashar's Treasure

"Now me!" said Ashar enthusiastically. "The treasure I want to bring and share, is Reflecting."

"Okay go for it Ashar," said Clara. "What does Reflecting mean and how has it helped you?"

"Well, Solomon talked about needing information and evidence when you're using his treasure, Reasoning, to help learn, solve problems and make decisions," said Ashar. "Reflecting is one of the ways you can get information and ideas to help you... and I've learned it's a particularly important way.

"Reflecting means stopping and taking a step back from what you are doing, and using that time to look, listen and think. When you do this, you'll find there are lots of new, helpful things to discover."

"Sounds intriguing," said Clara smiling, "tell us more."

"I grew up in a town called Falmouth," Ashar started, "in a happy family. I loved sports and being energetic. I won't give you my life story now, but here are the main things I've learned about Reflecting, and how it has helped me.

"All the things I've learned start with the first one:

"Stop .... take time to look and listen:

"When I was small, I was always on the move, rushing into everything without thinking. It often got me into trouble; my mum used to say I was like a bull in a china shop. Everyone was always telling me to stop, but I rarely did; there just wasn't time, and life was too exciting.

"The first time I remember realising that there was a benefit in stopping, was at the beach.

"I was running around, splashing in the water, and climbing on the rocks – I wanted my dad to join in, but he was just crouching down looking intently into a rock pool.

"I went to see what he was looking at, but I couldn't see anything. He said I had to just stay there, very still for a while and look carefully and for the first time in my life, I did. It took a few minutes, and I wanted to run off, but then I started to see things – tiny fish, little crabs, shrimps. I was amazed.

"I've come to realise that life is like that – if you don't just stop, take time, and pay attention, you miss lots of fascinating things … if you learn to stop, look, and listen, then lots of useful and interesting things reveal themselves.

"Stop and notice … pay attention to what is working and what isn't working:

"I used to love football. My dad liked football too and he encouraged us to make a little team of my friends. He used to help find other teams to play for fun.

"I was very competitive, so I wanted to be the best. I wanted to score the most goals and always be on the winning side, so I asked my dad how I could be the best. He just told me to do what the really good players did.

"I was annoyed. I couldn't see what the good players were doing that was different to me; I just wanted him to tell me what to do, so I could do it - but he wouldn't. Instead, he made me stop playing and just watch.

"I was mad for a while, but then he pointed out some things people were doing and after a while I did start noticing, not only what people were doing, but also what worked and what didn't work.

"I started to try doing more of the things that worked and less of the things that didn't work. Doing that made me pay more attention to what I was doing, rather than just rushing in trying to get the ball or a goal all the time.

"It was my first real experience of Reflecting. I found watching, noticing, and paying attention to what I was doing, or had done, helped me to gradually improve and I became a much better player.

"Stop and ask questions ... of yourself and others... to help you understand:

"One day my group of friends got into a huge row and fell out with each other big time!

"I didn't like it as I missed the fun we had together, so I wanted to sort it out. Even though I hadn't seen what had happened, I thought if they all just said sorry, everything would go back to normal, so I decided to tell them that was what they should do.

"Unfortunately, when I said that to them, they just got angry with me as well, so I asked my dad what to do.

"He got me to describe exactly what had happened, what I'd said and how they'd reacted. Then he asked me why I thought they'd been cross with me. When I thought about it, I guessed none of them wanted to say sorry, as none of them thought they were the ones who'd done anything wrong.

"Then my dad asked me if I understood why they were angry with each other in the first place. I realised I was so keen to sort it out, that I hadn't even stopped to ask myself if I really understood what the problem was.

"To cut a long story short, I realised I didn't really understand why they were so upset with each other, so I went to each of them, said sorry for being bossy, and then asked them to help me understand why they'd fallen out in the first place.

"By asking them why they thought they'd fallen out, and why they were so upset, it not only helped me to understand what had happened, but it made them ask that question of themselves and they started to understand better as well.

"They all had a slightly different story and now that they'd started to think more about what had happened, they stopped feeling so cross. They began to want to sort it out and realised it might be helpful to try and understand each other's points of view. When they talked and listened to each other they found it easier to say sorry and it didn't take long before they were friends again.

"There are lots of questions I've found it useful to ask myself like... 'Why am I doing this? Is that what I really wanted to do? Why am I upset? Did that go well? Why didn't that go well? What's really going on here? ... but before each of them you must stop ... and that brings me to my last one:

"Stop and pay attention to what your quiet self is saying:

"When I slowed down a bit and learned to stop more and reflect, I noticed that often I had a feeling, or a thought, gently prodding me from the inside.

"It sometimes asks the very questions I mentioned just now, or just sort of prods me about something I'm about to do and makes me know it isn't a good idea. At other times it gives me courage to do something good even though I'm unsure how it'll go, or makes me realise I'm uncomfortable about something someone is asking me to do and encourages me to say no.

"There are also times when it just makes me feel very calm and peaceful or bubbles with happiness and makes me realise how much I am enjoying something.

"I never even noticed it when I was rushing around, but when I stop and listen it's often there.

"I call it my 'quiet self'. It's always gentle, quiet, kind, brave and sort of wise. When I hear it and don't listen to it, I often later wish I had; like when it says 'don't leave that there or you'll forget it' - if I ignore it and do still leave whatever it was there ... I usually do forget it!

"I had that feeling when Solomon hurt his leg and had to be put ashore... I just felt inside that I needed to go with him, and I'm extremely glad I did.

"My quiet-self told me it was a good idea to stay here in Waterside when he was better, and I was thinking of going home cos there was nothing for me here... and it's telling me that being a Positive Pirate is a good idea for me... so here I am."

"You can see why it goes with my treasure," added Solomon, "it is always a good idea to stop, think and listen before doing most of the things I talked about."

"It goes really well with my treasure too," said Dante, "stop and notice how you are looking at things."

"... and mine," agreed Alik, "stop and notice what you are choosing."

"... and mine," said Phoebe excitedly, "stop and consider what you are trying to achieve."

"Well," said Clara, "for once I don't think we need to ask you how this can help others if we share it as Positive Pirates. It seems it adds something to each of our treasures that will make them even better.

"So, Ashar we would love you to be a Positive Pirate with us, and I am so glad your 'quiet self' told you to come along. What would you like your Positive Pirate nickname to be?"

"Well actually," said Ashar, "I quite like the name Pele. I met someone with that name once who was exceptionally good at football, and I remember thinking it was a cool name, so I'd like to choose that."

"Welcome Ashar, or Positive Pirate Pele," announced Clara, as the others gave the usual cheer.

Chapter 12: Clara's Treasure

"Thank you all so much for telling us about your treasures – and a bit about you," said Clara. "I hope when we are off sailing together, at some point it will be possible to hear more about each of your lives, as it's obvious you have interesting stories to tell.

"We have a lot to do to get ready for our first voyage, and I am very keen to see what Solomon and Ashar have brought in that box, but it doesn't seem fair to have asked you all to tell us about what you bring to being a Positive Pirate, without me doing the same. So, shall I tell you what I bring?"

"Yes of course," they all chorused.

"Is that okay Dad?" asked Clara, looking at Captain C. "It means sharing some things about your life too." He nodded his agreement.

"Well," started Clara, "I would say the treasure I bring is Aspiring. To me Aspiring means two things:

• it means looking at the future and deciding what you want to be and do; something different, something you think is better than you would otherwise be or do if you just went with the flow.

• then it means doing whatever is needed to become what you have chosen, over time.

"You can aspire to be anything really – you can aspire to be a certain kind of person, or to be successful at something in particular (like a certain kind of job), or to be better in some way, but aspiring requires a choice for the future and effort over time.

"These are the things that I have learned about being Aspiring, and how they've helped me:

"It's choosing what you want to be or do – not just letting things happen:

"As Alik said, at first, he didn't realise he was making choices.

"Aspiring is about making a choice –choosing to be or do something different than would otherwise happen. You can choose to just go with the flow and see what happens in life but that isn't Aspiring.

"As Bill has always told me 'If you do what you have always done, you will get what you have always got!' It might feel safe to go with the flow, but you can't be sure you won't look back later in life and wish you had chosen differently.

"My dad did that. His father and his grandfather had all been pirates and he just went with it too. He's told me there were times in his life when he realised it wasn't really who he wanted to be, but he carried on.

"When he came back here a few years ago he felt he'd wasted his life, mostly doing things he didn't really feel good about.

"Listening to him made me even more sure that I was going to choose what I want to be and do with my life … not just go with the flow.

"Thankfully, he has a few years in him yet, so he's got time to make different choices!

"Thinking about what I want to be or achieve:

"As I mentioned, there are lots of choices you could make about what you might aspire to become, but I found two things were important for me: finding what brought me joy and thinking about who I want to be in the future.

"I think your 'quiet self' often lets you know the things that bring you joy, but it's a good idea to take time to decide.

"When I was little, I liked the idea of doing lots of exciting things but, as I got older, I found that although I still liked them, they weren't that important to me.

"At one point I really wanted to be a dancer; I was always dancing around and begging Mary to get me lessons, but when

I first tried sailing, I forgot about dancing! Dancing was fun but sailing brought me joy.

"Sometimes other people notice things about who you are, and what you enjoy, more easily that you can.

"I found lots of activities I enjoyed, but Mary noticed that I was always talking to new people, finding out about their lives, and telling her how sad it was when life was so hard for people.

"She pointed it out to me, and I realised that, apart from sailing, out of all the things I was trying, the thing I wanted most was to see the world and do something to help make it a better place for more people, because I knew how wonderful life could be.

"I didn't know exactly what I would do straight away, but I knew it meant I would leave Waterside one day and do what I could to make a difference.

"Looking out for possibilities & opportunities … near and far:

"I'm lucky, I spent my first few years at sea, then in Waterside where we have so many different people from all over the world.

"I know not everyone sees that as good, but all the jobs I do have given me a chance to meet many of those people and hear about their lives. Without them, I would never have realised there are so many possibilities; different places to go and things I could do.

"I guess some people never look for possibilities, or try different things, and never realise they could choose to make their life different.

"My dad didn't consider how things could be different or explore other possibilities, until a few years ago, when he realised being a pirate wasn't making him happy or satisfied. When he thought about what he wanted to be, he thought of me, and decided his real aspiration was to be a better father to me, so he came back, and now he certainly is being that!

"When Dad found he had a ship going spare, I saw the possibilities and he supported me. That was when what I aspired for started to become a reality; for all of us!

"Sometimes you must wait for opportunities to become what you aspire for, but you must be ready to grab them when they come.

"Putting in the effort:

"Aspiring also means putting in the effort towards whatever you have chosen … it's not about just hoping things will turn out.

"Mary taught me this from gardening – she's extremely good at growing massive vegetables, but she doesn't just put a seed in the ground and hope for the best.

"She finds out what that plant likes and then makes sure it has all the things it needs to help it grow big; and she has to protect it from things that will damage it, like too much water, slugs, or greenflies.

"When I realised that part of what I aspired to was to leave Waterside and set sail, I knew I would need money, so that's the other reason I have two jobs – to save up money for my aspiration… and it's paid off. I had enough money to pay you all for three days to get the ship ready and decide if you want to be positive pirates.

Clara knew she wasn't finished there.

"The next question I've asked you all is why you think this is a treasure that's worth sharing as a Positive Pirate," she continued. "For me Aspiring is the reason why I invented the idea of Positive Pirates.

"Our world is beautiful – like a paradise; the main reason why it isn't a paradise all the time, is because of us people; the things we think and do - to ourselves, our world, and each other.

"We are the main reason why we are not all thriving and experiencing life in our world as something good.

"It makes me sad inside when I see what a mess we sometimes make of our beautiful world, and how bad we often are at caring for ourselves, it, and each other.

"My 'quiet self' wants to make a difference to that.

"I'm only one small person, but if we're going to make life better, and keep our world beautiful, then every small person needs to aspire to make a change, as does every big person!

"We need to change what we think about and do to ourselves; we need to change what we think about and do to the world, and we need to change what we think about and do to each other.

"Having listened to you all, those are exactly the things you want too and together we can make a start. The more people we can encourage to aspire to make a change, then the more hope we will all have for our world."

"Bravo!" they all cheered, even Rocco. "Welcome Positive Pirate Captain Clara!"

"Excellent – what a team!" said Clara beaming; then she turned to Solomon and Ashar.

"Now tell us what's in that box you two!"

"Cake!" said Solomon opening the box to reveal a huge chocolate cake. "We thought we might have a new team to celebrate, and it seems we were right... tuck in everyone!" ...and they did.

Chapter 13: Becoming a Team

The next morning everyone met up again on the ship to talk about next steps. Rocco was also hanging around a bit uncertainly, unsure if he was in or out.

"Welcome team!" beamed Clara. "We've got some important things to talk about, and a few problems to solve before we can set off on our first voyage. Before we get started though, I wanted to go back to those ideas you were all having yesterday, about different ways people could be part of what we're doing. I thought you made some really good points:

- Phoebe – you mentioned that some people want to give us other kinds of treasure to help us, even though they can't come along themselves.

- Ashar – you said some people might not yet know what treasures they have to offer, as they don't know what they're good at and maybe need some help with that.

- Dante – you said some people might just not be ready yet so the timing might not be right. It's true, it would be a shame if people missed out because there was only one chance to choose.

- Solomon – you pointed out that maybe some people aren't able to join us on a ship, or can't leave right now, and that some may want to come for just a short while rather than forever.

- Alik – you were right that we should give people choices about how they could contribute to what we're trying to achieve.

"I think you're right about all these things and I want us to keep them in mind as we make our plans. We need to find ways to offer people choices and chances to help us as often, and in as many ways, as we can. That brings me to you Rocco."

Clara turned to Rocco who was so taken aback he nearly fell backwards over a rope. Clara smiled.

"Sorry Rocco, I didn't mean to put you on the spot, but I seem to remember you said you might like to join us for one voyage and help us get started... is that still what you want?"

"Yes," said Rocco, trying not to look as embarrassed as he clearly was. "I do, but... well ... there's more to it than that." He stopped, seemingly unsure whether to say more.

"Go on," said Clara.

"The thing is," he said after a moment, "that first day when you told us about Positive Pirates, one of the sailors from another ship came up to me. He'd heard me talking and guessed where I'd come from, from my accent. He said he'd been in my home area not long ago and things weren't good. Apparently, there's hardly any food as the last harvest failed and there's a lot of sickness. If the harvest fails again, they'll be in real trouble."

"Oh, I see," said Clara "you must be worried?"

"Yes," he said sadly. "Like I said, I mostly became a pirate because I wanted to take back money to my family – to give them a better life, but the truth is I've never been able to send much. I haven't been home in years and hearing they might be in trouble made me realise how much I miss them. The more I think about it, the more I just want to go home, even if the harvest is good this year, and if it isn't I want to be there to help. Trouble is, my current Captain isn't willing to go that way and take me and, well, I was kind of hoping you might help me get some of the way home."

"Is your home near the sea Rocco?" asked Solomon.

"Not far from it," said Rocco, "that's how I got the idea of being a pirate – there's a natural harbour just down the coast, a couple of hours walk from the town. I know it's a lot to ask, but would you be willing to take me home, Captain ...? I could help out on the way, and I'd like to?"

"Captain," said Dante, sounding thoughtful and somewhat tentative, as he still wasn't quite sure how much Clara would welcome suggestions, "erm...maybe we could not only take Rocco home… but… if the harvest has failed … I wonder if maybe we could … try and help his hometown? Err… maybe we could try to find a way out of their problems? Maybe it could be a Positive Pirate mission?"

"That's a lot of maybes Dante!" teased Clara, but her tone was kind, "You don't need to sound so hesitant - Is it because you're not sure if I like you suggesting things?" Dante nodded sheepishly.

"Then I need to be clear with you all," continued Clara. "There will be times when, as the Captain, I'll have to make quick decisions because there isn't time to talk about it, and we just have to do something quickly. In those situations, you will just have to do what you're told, even if you disagree with the decision, or think it's not the best one. But, if there is time to discuss things and come to decisions together or look back and learn from a decision that didn't go so well, that is always what I prefer to do. To me that's part of being in a team and I want us to benefit from all our treasures. So, I'm incredibly happy for you to suggest things."

She looked at Dante who was looking relieved. "As for this suggestion Dante, it's a lovely idea, but, if the harvest has failed, it does sound like a huge challenge, especially for a new team."

She turned to the others, "We have time to discuss this, so it isn't just up to me; we're a team now. If we're going to take on this challenge then everyone needs to agree, not least you Rocco." She turned to Rocco, "Hopefully the harvest will have been good, but if not, we can't be sure we would be able to find a way out of the problems… what do you think … should we even offer to try? Do you think they would want our help?"

"I can't speak for them," said Rocco, "but I think it's brilliant you would even be willing to give it a try, so I can't believe my luck!" He looked around at everyone enthusiastically. "Yes of course I want you to give it a try! The leaders of my town might not like strangers knowing their business, but I'd do my best to persuade them… I'd be keen to try anything that might help. I know it'll be quite a while before we get there, but there's no way to get back there quickly anyway, so this is a great idea for me."

"Well, what do we think?" said Clara turning to the others. "Are we all willing to give it a try?"

"I agree it would be a huge challenge," said Solomon, "but I'm up for it, as long as we're realistic and honest about the fact that we don't have all the answers."

"Me too," added Ashar, "but Rocco's right that we'd need to make sure the local leaders were willing to work with us. Even if we did find a way to solve the problems, it would be them that would have to change and do new things and we couldn't make them do it."

"... No, they'll have to choose to make the changes!" agreed Alik, "I think it would be a wonderful start for us as well and I'm certainly up for helping them to make choices that will help them."

"Me too, "said Phoebe, "we can help them to become Resourceful!"

"...and Resilient!" added Dante cheerfully; he was confident now that he knew it was okay to make suggestions, but he noticed there was one person left who hadn't expressed an opinion.

He turned to Clara to ask. "So, the question is Captain Clara, are you up for it?" Clara smiled.

"If we do it, we'll all need your resilience Dante; this wouldn't be a quick mission and it could certainly be a huge challenge. I think...," Clara took a pause before she finished, and they all waited with bated breath. "I think it sounds like just the sort of thing we came together to do ... if the harvest has failed it might require all our treasures, but yes... I think we will take Rocco home and see what we find!"

"Yeah!" they all cheered, and Rocco forgot himself and did a short pirate jig for joy - he was going home!

Chapter 14: What Next?

N ow they had made their first big decision and had an idea what their first mission might be, Clara knew it was time to talk about some more difficult things they needed to focus on.

"I want to start by being honest about the challenges," she began. "I know some of you have noticed there are some bigger repairs that need to be done to the ship, and I know sorting them out will cost a lot more money than I have. That's probably our biggest challenge; we've found your treasures, now we need another kind of treasure too! Our other challenge is working out what we want to do to prepare for life at sea and for our missions as Positive Pirates." She stopped as she could see Phoebe wanted to say something as she was kind of bouncing. Clara beckoned to her to speak.

"I'm sorry to interrupt… but I think it might help, and it sounds like we need it!" said Phoebe excitedly. "I had some thoughts about the things you said you wanted us to keep in mind, about how to offer choices and chances for other people to be part of this."

"Go on…" invited Clara, aware they needed all the help they could get. Phoebe sat up purposefully.

"Well, we agreed there might be quite a few people who could help us in lots of different ways, with skills we need, or to share other kinds of treasures."

"That's true," said Ashar. "There were all those people who brought things to help us when you first told us all about Positive Pirates. I think there may be more people who might want to do that too but who didn't come that day; they might not have been free, or just weren't as curious as us."

"Yes, I see what you mean … so what are you suggesting?" asked Clara, interested in where this was going. It was Phoebe who picked it back up as she was always good at thinking about how to get people involved.

"Maybe we need to spread the word again," she said, "so that more people understand what we're aiming to do. At the same time, we could make it clear that we are willing to talk to people who may be interested in helping in other ways."

"That does make sense," said Clara, "what does everyone else think?"

"We do need to be a bit careful," reasoned Solomon. "What if we end up with more helpers than Positive Pirates, or being given lots of stuff that we really don't need, and none of the stuff we do need? Having said that though, it's good to have an open mind and see what opportunities arise."

"If there really are others who have stuff that they're happy to contribute," said Alik, "then we'd be stupid not to take it, as it could make a real difference."

"What's that saying?" said Dante with a grin on his face, "'Never look a gift horse in the mouth'? That certainly makes sense in this situation... not that we need horses of course!"

"True…" laughed Clara, "we need some way to separate the gifts from the horses I guess … so we can fit it all on the ship!" For some reason, her thoughts turned to Frank, but she pushed the thought aside… she suspected having him on the ship would have been a bit like having a horse on board.

"Well, joking aside," she continued quickly, "it seems we all agree we definitely need more help and resources, but Solomon's right that we need to be careful not to have lots of people and things we don't need. I suppose there are lots of ways people could possibly get involved and help. Phoebe, were you also saying you think some people still don't understand what we're trying to achieve?"

"Yes, I am," said Phoebe. "I know there are lots of people who haven't heard about it at all, and others who don't understand about having treasures and using them to help others and make the world a better place."

"It would certainly be a shame if we went sailing off to do that," said Clara thoughtfully, "whilst the people back in our hometown didn't even understand what being a Positive Pirate really was. I'm also sure we aren't the only ones who have treasures either."

"People sometimes understand better if they see something in action," said Ashar, "rather than just having it explained."

"Yes of course," said Clara, "did you have an idea how we could do that?"

"Not exactly," Ashar replied. "I'm just thinking that if we want to help them understand, then the best way might be to show them what using your treasures can do."

They all thought for a while.

"We could do a project!" said Alik, suddenly excited. "We could show them what we as a team can do with our treasures."

"Oooh, I like that idea," said Clara. "Do you have an idea for a project?"

"Not yet, "admitted Alik, "but I'm sure we could come up with one if we had a bit of time."

"Okay thinking caps on everyone and let us know when you come up with any ideas!" said Clara cheerfully. "In the meantime, we need to get on with working out what we need to do to get the ship sorted, especially with no money. We're going to need all kinds of help. Has anyone got any other ideas about how we solve Solomon's problem of getting the stuff we actually need to help us?"

"Well..." said Phoebe thoughtfully, "the project will help of course, but I think we also need a simple way to get people thinking about the actual ship and wanting to help get it ready."

"I agree," said Solomon, "but we'll have to do some thinking about what we actually need to get done on the ship first, so that we know what to ask for!"

"Yes, you're right," said Phoebe, "but while we do that, I'm wondering what will make people want to help. Our ship doesn't even have a name yet and it's hard to get people excited about something that doesn't even have a name! I'm wondering if having a naming ceremony might help people get excited. It'll take some time to plan one, but people love a naming ceremony!"

"Brilliant! Yes of course ... that's reminded me, that was something I wanted to talk to you all about" agreed Clara. "I think the name of the ship is really important. I had some ideas about names, but I wanted us to agree it together. If we do that then of course a naming ceremony would be just the thing to get people excited about helping us sort the ship out. I wanted us to choose a name that would reflect our mission; shall I tell you my ideas?"

"It might be difficult not to just choose one you come up with," said Alik bravely, as he didn't want to upset Clara, "since you're the Captain! I'm not saying your ideas won't be good, but you did say we are a team, and you want us to discuss ideas when we can. Maybe we could collect everyone's ideas before we decide – without knowing who they belong to. If we don't know who's they are it might be easier to be honest when we don't like one."

"Good point Alik!" agreed Clara, feeling a bit guilty for getting carried away with her own ideas. "How about we put all our ideas in a box by tomorrow – then we can pick one out and that will be the name. Dante, if you don't feel confident writing, I am sure one of the others will be happy to do it with you."

Dante smiled and nodded his agreement, but Solomon looked doubtful.

"I think we need to be a bit careful about just picking a name out of a box," he said. "What happens if we pick one out that really isn't any good – we don't want to be stuck with it!"

"Oh! I'm so relieved you said that Solomon!" said Clara. "I do want you all to have a say, but at the same time I really care about what name we choose." There was silence for a moment while they all considered what to do. Everyone knew it was important to get it right.

"We could read all the suggestions out and then each vote secretly for the four we like the best," suggested Alik, "if one comes out top then we'll have a decision."

"What happens if there isn't one with a top score?" asked Phoebe. "Or if the top one is one Clara really doesn't like? It does feel important that she, out of all of us, likes the name we end up with."

"I don't want to seem more important than the rest of you though," said Clara uncertainly, "but I must admit it's true, it does really matter to me what the ship is called."

"How about we allow Clara to look at the names that come out top from the voting," proposed Solomon, "and she can either choose one she likes best, if she has a favourite, or put all the ones she doesn't mind having back in the box and we will pull one of those out … and that will be the name!"

"A very reasoned approach," smiled Ashar. "I think we should do it that way but then, maybe when the final name comes out, Clara gets a chance to change her mind. She needs to be able to listen to what her quiet self is saying… and I find sometimes you don't realise what you really wanted, until you get something else and feel disappointed!" he laughed.

"Too true my reflective friend, good idea!" smiled Solomon. "So, if Clara suddenly realises her quiet self is not happy with the final name, then we try again." Everyone was happy.

"It's a deal then," said Clara, confident this would work. "Name ideas in the box and we choose first thing tomorrow. Then, Phoebe, we need to come up with a way to get lots of people interested in the naming ceremony and helping with the ship."

"Leave that to me and Alik," said Phoebe, "we know lots of local people. When the time comes maybe we can get someone important, like the Mayor, to break a bottle on the boat in true launching style! We'll need a name plate, and a flag of course…"

"I'd love to help with the design," offered Dante, "although of course I wouldn't be any good at doing the writing. Maybe Rocco can help with the writing as he is very neat." Rocco nodded and smiled bashfully.

"Deal!" said Clara happily. "Now we need to give some more thought to what we need for the ship." She turned to Ashar and Solomon. "You two are good at thinking things through. Perhaps you could help me work out how we can do this, so we don't end up with lots of people and things being offered that we have to say no to?"

"Absolutely" they both said in unison.

A suggestion box was put on the table, and they all went off to get on with their tasks, agreeing to come together again the next morning to see what ideas they had come up with.

Chapter 15: Choosing

By the time they came together the next morning a lot had been achieved. Phoebe and Alik had thought about the naming ceremony and how it could work, Dante had measured up the rough size for the name plate and had started drawing some designs for that and the flag, and Clara, Ashar and Solomon had some ideas about how to do it all in a way that would avoid making people feel rejected, if what they had to offer was not really needed at the moment.

They'd all been coming up with possible names for the ship, and even some ideas about what their team project could be, but everyone knew the first thing was choosing the ship's name.

They all gathered around the suggestion box. The good news was, that when they shook the box, they could hear there were quite a few suggestions inside. Solomon and Ashar had brought enough pens for each of them, so they could vote; even Rocco was allowed a vote which made him feel special. It felt a bit like Christmas as Clara opened the box to see what was inside.

There were quite a lot of suggestions and Clara read each one out carefully and placed them all in a long line across the side of the room to make it easier to see them all for voting. Rocco helped Dante when he wasn't sure about what they said, but his reading was already improving well. They all had four votes and used a tick to give their votes to the suggestions they liked the best.

When the votes were counted, and double checked, there were three names that had a lot more votes than the rest, and the number of votes were so close that there wasn't really anything between them:

'Hope Bringer'   'World Saver'   'The Difference'

They all looked at Clara to see if she had a favourite.

Unfortunately, the only thing going through Clara's mind at that moment, was the realisation that this was really important, and she must make the right decision. She had no idea what her 'quiet self' was telling her about the names. All she could feel was panic that she might make the wrong decision and let everyone down; consequently, her mind had gone completely blank.

The time ticked by, and it didn't get any better… everyone was looking at her expectantly and she felt very silly after making all that fuss about wanting to choose, because now she had no idea! In the end she knew she had to say something, so she decided the best thing was to just follow the process Solomon had suggested.

"I don't think I have a preference," she told the others rather uncertainly, "so let's put all three in a hat and I'll just pick out one and that will be the name!"

Dante folded each of them carefully and put them into a hat for Clara to take one out. He could see that something was wrong, but he wasn't sure what. Ashar had noticed too.

"Clara, whatever choice you make we'll all be happy with it, and we'll make it work," said Dante reassuringly, "they're all good names so none of them will be 'wrong', whatever you choose. Try not to look at it as a right or wrong decision."

"Thank you, Dante," said Clara, feeling a little better, "it does feel like a big pressure – you're right though, I'm looking at this the wrong way - all of these names are good, so I can't make a bad decision!"

Ashar had some advice too. "Just take a deep breath and notice how you feel when you read the one that comes out. Trust your quiet self to tell you if it's not really the one you want."

Clara took a deep breath, breathed out slowly, then put her hand in and pulled out a folded paper. She opened it and rather shakily read out the words "World Saver".

There was silence for a long moment. Ashar was about to ask her what she felt when she spoke.

"Actually Ashar … you were right," said Clara. "Reading this I find I'm a bit disappointed. I realise now that I wanted 'Hope

Bringer' to come out." As soon as she said this, Clara felt her confidence start to flood back, "Yes, now I'm sure ... our ship is called 'Hope Bringer'! Hope is the light that guides us towards what we believe is the best for us ... our best life and our best world... it's our purpose in two words!"

They all clapped and cheered – they had a name and what a good name it was. Positive Pirates were about bringing hope and they would be setting sail on the Hope Bringer. Everyone was happy and sure it was the best choice.

When they'd finished cheering, someone suggested they ought to ask Solomon to make another cake to celebrate, until Alik pointed out, that if they made a habit of eating cake each-time they did something they were happy about, then they would soon become very unhealthy.

"Okay," laughed Clara, "no more cake for the moment but there will be plenty of cake, and lots of other scrumptious things at our naming ceremony!" That was an idea everyone liked.

"Now we know our ship's name, we need to think about spreading the word," continued Clara, "did anyone have any ideas about what our team project could be?"

Alik and Phoebe looked at each other and nodded. It was Phoebe who spoke.

"Yes, actually we think we might have just the right idea," she said dramatically. "It came to us when we were thinking about the naming ceremony for the ship. Obviously, it will be in the harbour, and there's is a bit of a problem with the harbour ... one the Mayor is always complaining about!"

"You mean how smelly and mucky it is!" said Dante who thought the Mayor had a point, having lived near a harbour that was much nicer.

"Exactly," said Alik, "showing how we could share our treasures as a team to help clean up the harbour would be a wonderful project. We think lots of people will be interested so it should spread the word, as well as make everyone happy, especially the Mayor."

"Plus, it would make our naming ceremony much nicer," finished Phoebe. "It's the perfect project!"

"No-one could say being shy about coming forward was one of your weaknesses Phoebe," laughed Clara, "but that's one of the things we love about you. I'm glad the two of you were working together as I have to agree it is a great idea. What do the rest of you think?" Everyone looked keen.

"It does seem perfect if we can pull it off," said Solomon. "Are we sure we can? I know 'believing you can' is one of your things Phoebe, but we need to be realistic."

"We'll need the townsfolk to help," agreed Alik, "but I think we can do it if we work together."

"As it's one of the Mayor's pet peeves, I'm sure he'll help get folk on board," said Clara. "I'll ask Bill and Mary the best way to get in touch with the Mayor and explain our idea; if we want him to make the naming ceremony a big occasion, we need to be sure he's 'on-board' with the idea!"

"Very funny!" said Solomon, then he added thoughtfully, "We'll just need to think of a way to do it that helps people understand about treasures. I'll have a think about how."

Chapter 16: The Mayor

That evening Clara told her family about the name they had chosen, and how they wanted to get the Mayor to come and do the naming ceremony. Everyone loved the name, and Bill, who as the Harbourmaster often had dealings with the Mayor, promised to get Clara a meeting with him to discuss her idea.

The next afternoon a leak had got a bit worse in the hold of the ship. Dante and Ashar were busy emptying buckets and mopping up the water, whilst Clara and Solomon were trying to work out the best way to fix it for the moment, when Bill rushed up to them, looking a bit stressed.

"Found you at last!" he said, getting his breath back. "The Mayor has agreed to come and meet you. He wants to come and see the ship."

"Does he like the idea of Positive Pirates?" asked Clara excitedly. Bill's face fell.

"Not exactly," he admitted. "I'm afraid he seems to have missed the whole thing completely! It seems he's been busy on other things, so he didn't hear about your announcement, and he hadn't even noticed the ship in the harbour. He was actually a bit put out that I hadn't told him before about my decision to let a 'ship like that' into the harbour. I'm sorry, I didn't even think of it!"

"Oh dear, it's not your fault," said Clara, "I'm sorry if we've got you into trouble. How did you get him to agree to do the naming ceremony?"

"That's just it," said Bill, looking even more crestfallen, "he hasn't ... but on the bright side he seems very keen to come and see the ship. He wants to come this afternoon – in less than an hour's time!"

Clara suddenly realised why Bill had been looking stressed.

"This isn't really a good time," she said looking around her, "we've got this leak and the ship's very messy as we've just dumped loads of stuff everywhere while we were planning what to do!"

"Nothing I can do about it I'm afraid!" said Bill, "I tried to put him off, but when he gets an idea in his head there's no stopping him. It's now or never if you want to get him on board!"

Solomon looked up from inspecting the leaky boards.

"I wish everyone would stop making that joke," he said, "it's going to get tired very quickly." Bill looked at him blankly, as did Clara.

"I don't think anyone was joking this time, Solomon mate!" said Ashar, "I think you need to notice the gravity of the situation. There's a bit of a crisis going on here!"

Solomon, who'd been paying more attention to the leak than the conversation, looked around at the mess and it began to dawn on him what Ashar was worried about.

"Maybe this needn't be a bad thing," suggested Dante, "it's not the ship we need him to like, it's the idea of Positive Pirates… and we could do with some help with the ship; there's no point in pretending that isn't the situation!"

Clara calmed down. "Thanks Dante," she said, "as usual you have a better way of looking at things. Okay, we'll show him things as they are. Hopefully, the idea will speak for itself."

So it was that half an hour later, Bill was introducing Clara to the Mayor. They were about to show him around the ship, having failed to persuade him to go in the house and have a cup of tea first, so that Clara could explain about Positive Pirates in more comfortable surroundings.

"I must say it's rather tatty-looking Bill," said the Mayor, who seemed to be having trouble taking in the fact that Clara was the captain. Annoying though it was, Clara was getting used to dealing with this; she knew she needed to take the lead, so the Mayor saw it was her in charge, not Bill.

"Looks can be deceiving," she said pointedly. "It's true she does need some work doing on her, but her structure is sound, and we think she'll make an excellent Positive Pirate ship. We're extremely lucky to have her!"

"Well yes, ships don't grow on trees, so I suppose you are!" said the Mayor who was secretly a little impressed with Clara's confidence but didn't want to show it.

"We certainly couldn't have hoped to launch Positive Pirates if we didn't have a ship," Clara continued, determined to keep mentioning Positive Pirates until the Mayor asked about them. "Although of course positive pirate treasures can be used anywhere."

The Mayor knew when he'd been beaten.

"I see you're not going to let me get away without hearing about all this pirate nonsense!" he said provocatively. "I can't imagine how you managed to persuade my Harbourmaster here to have a pirate ship in the harbour when he knows it is against the rules, even if you are his daughter!"

"There are no rules about Positive Pirates!" said Bill, joining in on the act with a smile in his eyes. "Go on Clara you'd better explain."

"I think maybe you had!" said the Mayor, sounding for all the world as if it had been his idea to hear about them all along.

Clara told him how it was her aspiration to start Positive Pirates and explained the difference between ordinary and positive pirates as she had done when she first did her announcement. The Mayor listened but his face didn't give anything away.

"A lofty aspiration certainly," he said after a moment, "helping others and making the world a better and happier place, no-one could disagree with that. I still don't understand what treasures you are talking about though. By the looks of this ship, it certainly isn't money!"

"You're right there," agreed Clara. "To be honest we could do with a little more of that kind of treasure at the moment, just to get the ship in shape. Perhaps the best way to explain the treasure

I am referring to, is for you to come and meet the crew. They can tell you about their treasures better than I can."

The Mayor nodded his agreement and beckoned for her to lead the way to her cabin where everyone was waiting; everyone except Rocco who was elsewhere that day. Clara was secretly glad he wasn't there, as clearly the Mayor was going to take a bit of convincing that they weren't all just ordinary pirates in disguise. They hadn't had time to clean themselves up after trying to sort the leak out, so they looked a bit tatty and dirty themselves... Clara hoped they could help the Mayor see past this.

Clara introduced each pirate by name, and nickname, saying they would each explain their treasure. The Mayor clearly recognised a few, especially Phoebe, but that didn't surprise anyone as she seemed to know everyone.

"I might have known you would be here young lady," he said to Phoebe, "you seem to get everywhere! What is your 'treasure' supposed to be then?"

Phoebe smiled her broadest smile. "My treasure is resourcefulness. It means I am good at finding ways to get what is needed in order to succeed at whatever we want to achieve."

"Mmm, I guess that rings true from what I know of you," said the Mayor, "so, how is you being like that going to help others and make the world a better place?"

"It's what I bring to the team," explained Phoebe, "so I help us as a team to find the resources we need to do the things we want to achieve. Then I hope to share my treasures with others and help them learn to be resourceful too."

"Huh, I'd like to see how your resourcefulness is going to help your team mend this ship and get it ready to sail!" said the Mayor a bit dismissively. Phoebe was ready for him.

"Part of being resourceful is knowing when you need help," she said confidently, "and who to ask. Maybe you are one of the people we need help from."

The Mayor looked a bit taken aback, but not in an angry way. Dante decided to help out.

"I'm Dante, or Positive Pirate Pavel, and my treasure is Resilience," he reminded the Mayor. "Part of being resilient is sticking at things when they're difficult. I think we're having a bit of difficulty persuading you of the value of our treasures, and funnily enough, we were just saying yesterday, how we thought that was something we needed to do for other people too… help them understand why these kinds of treasures are valuable."

Clara realised where Dante was going with this, and decided it was time she helped out too.

"Yes," she said brightly, "we had an idea about how we could demonstrate our treasures in action. A way in which sharing our treasures could help to make Waterside a better place."

"I'd certainly like to hear about that!" said the Mayor.

"We thought it might be good to show how sharing our treasures could help clean up the harbour and make it nicer for everyone!" said Clara, with her fingers crossed behind her back, hoping it was as good an idea as they thought it was.

The Mayor's faced brightened.

"That would certainly go down well," he said thoughtfully, "and not just with me… but do you really think you can pull that off?"

"Yes, we do!" said Clara confidently, her fingers still crossed behind her back; she knew it was a risk, but it seemed worth taking and she knew the others agreed. The Mayor didn't think about it for long.

"Well, if you can really help me with that," he said, still sounding a little doubtful, "then I suppose I can try to find a way to help you with your problem." He looked over at Phoebe, who smiled broadly.

"Then it's a deal!" said Clara and they shook hands on it.

Solomon watched with a mixture of happiness and anxiety. Like the rest of the team, he was very pleased the Mayor had gone for their suggestion, but he remembered his promise to come up with an idea about how to do it and at the moment he didn't have one. He knew how important it was that the project was a success, but the more he tried to think of an idea the blanker his brain seemed to become.

After everyone had left, he talked to Ashar about his problem.

"I suggest you go and cook something," said Ashar, who knew his friend well. "Cooking seems to relax you, and you always seem to be telling me ideas you've come up with when you're cooking. I think ideas come more easily when you're relaxed. it's worth a try anyway!" Solomon agreed.

Chapter 17: Treasures Together

The next day the Mayor was off doing other important stuff, and the team, including Rocco, sat down together to talk about how they would do the Harbour Project. There was quite a buzz, as most of them were excited at the prospect, but Dante noticed Rocco wasn't his usual enthusiastic self.

"What's up Rocco?" he asked, "don't you like the idea of the Harbour Project?"

"It's not that. It's nothing really," he said in a tone that made it even more clear something was the matter. "It's not my business really."

Hearing this Clara knew she couldn't let it pass.

"We're a team," she said, "and while you're with us, you are part of the team too ... so it is your business. Please tell us, and we'll decide together if it's really 'nothing.'"

"Okay," sighed Rocco, giving in easily, "I'm just a bit worried that's all. It seems to me that if you do this project, it'll be even longer before we're ready to leave. I'm just keen to get home in case things haven't improved."

"That's a fair point," said Clara, "of course you're worried, but hopefully their harvest will be good so things will have got better. Anyway, to be honest, there's a lot to do to get the ship, and ourselves, ready, but it will take even longer if we don't get the help we need. We're hoping that doing this will help people understand what Positive Pirates are and encourage them to give us at least some of the help we need. If it works, it should make things quicker."

"Surely the project shouldn't mean us doing most of the work," said Alik, "we're meant to be showing people what we mean by treasures and how they can be valuable, not doing everything ourselves!"

"Okay," said Rocco, looking a bit more cheerful. "What exactly is this Harbour Project anyway?"

"Good question." said Phoebe, "I've been thinking, we need to be really clear what we're aiming to achieve… and if we want to show off all our treasures, we'll need the whole team involved somehow. Then, to cap it all, we need to do it in a way that clearly shows how each of our treasures is helping."

"That is quite a challenge!" agreed Clara. "Has anyone got any ideas? Solomon, you said you'd try and come up with an idea, did you have any success?"

Ashar looked at his mate who he knew had been shut away in the pub kitchen most of the previous evening. He hoped his cooking idea had worked, but he hadn't had time to ask. He'd noticed that Solomon didn't seem so stressed this morning, so he hoped that meant he did have an idea ready.

"I spend yesterday evening in the kitchen cooking," said Solomon, as if he'd read Ashar's mind, "and it struck me that maybe it's a bit like baking a cake." The others looked at him a little puzzled, but Ashar smiled, it seemed his idea had worked; Solomon always relaxed when he was cooking, and it was when he was relaxed that he always had the best ideas.

"Our treasures are like the ingredients needed in the recipe," continued Solomon. "Maybe we tell them the Harbour Project a bit like baking a Harbour Cake, a cake with several different flavoured layers. Each stage of the project is like a new layer of the cake and will need to use a different mix of ingredients, a different mix of our treasures, to make it. When we put all the layers together, we'll end up with a delicious Harbour Cake – or rather a lovely harbour!"

Whilst the others were taking in the idea Ashar caught Solomon's eye and gave him a thumbs up; it was a good idea. It didn't take long for the others to agree with him.

"I like that way of looking at it," said Dante, grinning. "Different ingredients for different types of cake and then of course the icing in-between the layers and on top. It sounds delicious!"

"That is very clever Solomon!" said Clara. "Thank you for coming up with the idea. Have you thought any more about how our Harbour Cake could work exactly?"

"Not yet," said Solomon, "it was just a thought. Like Alik said, somehow, we need to make sure our treasures, the ingredients, are in the mix without necessarily being in the bowl ourselves."

There was silence for a few minutes – some people were thinking about the problem but, looking round, Clara wondered if others were thinking more about cake! It was Ashar who broke the silence.

"How about we decide which ingredients are needed at each stage in the recipe and how they need to be used," he said, "then actually get them to do the work of using them, instead of us."

"That's brilliant," said Alik, "it means it's them doing the mixing... and the work, so they get to experience using the treasures and working together!"

"Ooh yes," said Phoebe, who rather liked making cakes too, "they'll have their fingers in the cake mix! I guess like with any cake, there'll be some ingredients you need a lot of, and others that are like seasoning, you just need a taste of them for flavour."

"Yes," agreed Solomon. "I've learned that with any form of cooking it's good to taste it as you go along and sometimes you need a little extra something to make it taste just right; the trick is knowing what that something is, and putting just the right amount in."

"So, you mean there might be some ingredients we don't think we need in one part of the recipe," said Clara, "but we might find, as we're actually making it, that we do need to add it."

"Like resilience," said Dante, "I'm not sure you would expect it to be one of the main ingredients in any of the layers but, if things get tough, that's exactly when we need to add it!"

"Or it might be the cherry on the top," said Ashar laughing, "when we look back after we've made it, we might realise we are more resilient than we thought, because we stuck at it when it was hard!"

"Very clever," said Clara, "we'll do some planning about which of our treasure ingredients we think we need for each layer."

"Maybe we could make a recipe card for each layer," suggested Alik, "to help people remember what ingredients they need and how to use them."

"Yes, good idea," said Clara. "I think together we can make this work really well. While we get on with the planning, I'll ask the Mayor to get people together so we can set them going to make their own Harbour Cake!"

"Can we have a cake to celebrate?" said Rocco hopefully.

Chapter 18: The Recipe

So it was that, a week later, they were in the Town Hall with the Mayor and a great crowd of people.

The team looked around, both nervous and excited. They were ready with their recipe idea, and knew the ingredients they needed for each stage, but they also knew that anything could happen, so they might sometimes need ingredients they hadn't expected. Harbour Cake was no ordinary cake, and they weren't sure anyone had ever made one before.

The Mayor had done a great job at getting a good mix of a lots of different people along, rich, and poor, representing lots of different groups who used the harbour, or lived near it. Many of them weren't really that sure why they were there, but the Mayor was an especially important person in the town, and if he told you to come along, people tended to come.

Clara could see the Mayor talking rather seriously with a group of important looking people over on one side of the Hall. He saw her looking, stopped the conversation and came over to the platform where the team were. It was quite noisy as everyone was talking amongst themselves, asking each other if they knew what was going on.

"Welcome everyone," said the Mayor in his loudest and most commanding voice. The noise died down as everyone strained to hear what he was going to say. He continued once there was hush.

"I am proud of this town. Waterside is a wonderful place to live, and I am very honoured to be your Mayor!" There was a murmur of approval. "However, as you all know there is one thing in this town that I am not proud of, and neither should any of you be!" He pointed menacingly round the hall as he said this.

The murmur of approval shifted into one of puzzlement and then silence. Everyone was hoping he wasn't talking about something to do with them.

"Our harbour is a disgrace!" he stated vehemently. "It should be the jewel in our crown, a place for everyone to enjoy, a place we could bring people to show them why we are proud to be called Waterside, but instead it is a disgusting mess, the stench of which can be smelled all the way from the Town Hall. I am ashamed, and so should we all be!"

"Hear, Hear!" shouted several voices in agreement, many of them from the group the Mayor had been talking to.

"Well," continued the Mayor, "the time has come for us to do something about it. I know some of you have heard of Clara and her team of Positive Pirates." He gestured towards Clara and the team and there was a cheer from a few people who did already know about them. The Mayor continued.

"I must admit that I hadn't heard of them till last week and I have still to be convinced about how pirates can ever be positive!" he said rather rudely. "However, as your Mayor I never miss an opportunity to do good things for our town, and they have told me that they can help us with our harbour problem. I don't know if that is true, but I have agreed to bring you together and give them this chance to show us what they're made of, by helping us to get this problem sorted once and for all. Over to you Positive Pirate Captain Clara!" He said her title with a slightly sarcastic tone.

This wasn't quite the enthusiastic introduction Clara and the team had been hoping for. The cheer from the few people who had known about them was small and short lived. As they had suspected, a lot of people hadn't and were just as sceptical as the Mayor. His rather unhelpful introduction had left everyone silent and unsure what to expect. The hush that greeted Clara when she stepped forward to speak was quite intimidating.

"I know the Mayor, and many of you, find the idea of Positive Pirates a difficult one," she started.

"You're right there!" came a stern voice from the group the Mayor had been talking to earlier. A few others said "Hear, hear!" in agreement.

Clara carried on, speaking as loudly and confidently as she could. "I understand that. Pirates are known for hurting and killing people to steal their treasure and that is certainly not a positive thing. Yet we all know that many people become pirates because they hear about the good things, about how they work together, look after each other and share out the treasures they find between them equally – these are positive qualities that we aim to demonstrate too."

There was a slight murmur of approval, then silence.

"Yet there is one other very important difference between us," Clara continued, "and it is about what we consider to be treasure. Unlike all other pirates we do not see treasures as gold and jewels, or valuable things that others have, which are there to be stolen; we see the skills and qualities we already have as our treasures, and we want to use and share them to make life better wherever we can."

Again, a slight murmur of approval. Clara pressed on.

"We know everyone has that kind of treasure, even though some people don't realise they do. As Positive Pirates we not only aim to share our own treasures, but also, when we can, we aim to help other people to discover the treasures they already have. We hope that we can all learn how to share our treasures and make the world a better place."

The silence prevailed but somehow it didn't feel quite as intimidating as before. Clara was about to continue when she noticed the Mayor stepping forward again.

"That all sounds incredibly good in theory," he said in a rather unhelpfully dismissive way, "but what are these mysterious treasures and how are you going to use them to help us with our harbour problem?"

"Thank you, Mayor, that is the question I guess you all want answered," said Clara. "We are a new team, in fact the whole idea of Positive Pirates is new, so you could say we are Practicing Positive

Pirates, (a few people tittered) but we feel the best place for us to start is in our home-town. If we can't make things better here, then we might struggle out there in the big wide world. That's why we want to work with you and share our treasures, to try to make a difference to our harbour problem."

The murmur of approval was much louder now and even the Mayor seemed to nod slightly. Clara kept going.

"Let me introduce you to the team. Many of us have lived in Waterside for all of our lives so we know many of you, and you know some of us, but not all, and we have Positive Pirate nicknames. We haven't been a team for long, and this is our first project, so we're still learning how our treasures work together. Please forgive us if we're a bit nervous, as seeing you all together like this, you're a big crowd so we may come across a bit like Wobbly Positive Pirates to start with!" Clara said this last bit whilst wobbling to make her point.

Everyone laughed. The ice was broken. The team were relieved as none of them were looking forward to talking in front of such a big crowd, and all this silence was making it even more scary. Phoebe however, who was rarely backwards in coming forwards, decided she would go first and try to help Clara out with a bit more humour. She stepped forward.

"Hi, I'm Positive Pirate Polly, better known to you as Phoebe, and I reckon there aren't many people here who haven't come across me at some time!" she started. There were shouts of "Too true!" around the room, but they were affectionate. She carried on, "I guess some of you might say I'm just nosey (laughter rippled round the room) but I believe my treasure is Resourcefulness, which means being good at finding ways to get what you need in order to succeed at whatever you want to achieve. I know I've helped some of you in the past, and certainly many of you have helped me and my family, but I'll tell you more about what it means and how it can help with this later."

There was a cheer from some of Phoebe's neighbours and a few people started to clap. Clara clapped too and in no time at all everyone joined in. Phoebe took a dramatic bow and the clapping got even louder; Phoebe was right, everyone did know her, and whilst yes, they might think she was a bit nosey sometimes, they also knew she was always helpful and kind.

Things after that were a lot easier for the others as they each received the same applause when they went up and introduced themselves. Everyone even clapped when Clara introduced Rocco and explained that he had joined them to find out what his treasure was, so he didn't have a Positive Pirate nickname yet. Clara was secretly rather relieved, as she was worried some might not be as accepting of an actual pirate, especially one who was naturally so rough and scary looking; looks could sometimes be deceiving, but she knew not everyone was good at looking past them.

Once the clapping was over the Mayor was there again wanting to move things on.

"So, how are you going to use these treasures of yours then?" he said, still sounding less than convinced, but a little less rude than before.

"We've thought about that," said Clara, "and we've come up with a way of looking at this that we hope will help you all. We thought that solving our harbour problem is a bit like baking a cake!"

"Typical woman – cooking on the brain!" said a loud voice, followed by laughter around the room.

"Actually, it was my idea!" said Solomon stepping forward. "Even if you don't all make cakes, I'm sure most of us have seen what it takes … and enjoyed licking the spoon afterwards!" There was cheerful agreement around the room. Clara signalled for Solomon to continue.

"We thought our treasures are like the ingredients – and each stage of solving the harbour problem is like making another layer of the cake. The Harbour Cake will have different flavoured layers and icing in between, so we will need a different mix of ingredients each time." You could hear people were getting into the idea round the room as people were making interested sounds.

"Remember though," Solomon continued, "it is our treasures that are the ingredients, not us. We will be sharing them with you, so that you can use them to make exactly the cake you want. We don't want to hold on to our treasures, we want you to have and use them to make Waterside Harbour Cake the best cake around!"

A cheer went up. Solomon beamed – his idea had worked even better than he had hoped, and it certainly felt nice to have got everyone cheering. The Mayor looked a little peeved it wasn't him getting the applause, but he wanted the harbour sorted so he nodded. Clara stepped forward.

"Are you ready to hear about the first ingredients?" she asked.

"Yes" came the loud reply.

Chapter 19: Harbour Cake Mix

They'd all agreed that Solomon should start the process, as the cake had been his idea and he was the best cake baker amongst them. "The first part of the recipe for Harbour Cake is the layer the rest of the cake will stand on," he explained, "so it needs to be firm as well as flavourful."

"Its main ingredients are Clara's treasure, Aspiration, and Ashar's treasure, Reflection," Solomon continued, "so I'm going to ask them to come and tell us how we can use their treasures here. Ashar first." Ashar stepped forward.

"As the Mayor said," started Ashar, "the harbour is 'a disgusting smelly mess', but we need to find out a bit more about what's wrong before we try to put it right. This is where Reflection comes in."

There was a buzz of conversation in the hall and people started to put their hands up and shout out to tell Ashar what was wrong with the harbour. Ashar raised his hand to quieten them, but it took the Mayor to shout loudly at them before they quietened down and listened again. Ashar continued.

"I know you have ideas already, but Reflection is about stopping and noticing things – when you stop and take time, you often notice things you haven't noticed before and that is what I want you to do. Not now, but before we come back together again, I want you to think about the harbour, or even better, go there, and to stop and notice exactly what isn't working. Work out why it's disgusting to you particularly? What are the smells you don't like, what is the mess, or is there something else that we haven't mentioned that doesn't please you? You might all notice different things and that is fine."

"Okay," said Solomon, "so, to put Reflection into the cake we need you to stop and notice the things you think are wrong with the harbour – these are the things we will want to get away from. Now let's hear from Clara about our other ingredient, Aspiration, which looks at what we want to move towards."

"Thank you," said Clara. "Unlike Ashar's treasure, which you need to take away and take a bit of time to use, we can start adding in Aspiration right here. The first part of Aspiration is thinking about what you want the future to be like." Clara had a plan for the next bit, so she carried straight on.

"I want you to get into groups of people you know and have something in common with. Maybe some fishermen together, some people who are neighbours, some shop keepers on the high street. Once you are in your group then stop talking and listen up again, and I will tell you what to do."

It took a while, and quite a bit of help from the whole team, but once people had got into groups Clara continued.

"So, to put the first Aspiration' ingredient in, I want each group to talk about what you want the harbour to be like when our problem is solved. What will the finished harbour be like? It can be things that are the same as now, or things you want to be different, but Aspiration is about what you want so I want to hear what you DO want, not what you DON'T want. You'll need someone in the group to tell me at the end what your group came up with, so decide who has the loudest voice first, then make sure everyone has a chance to say what they think."

The noise from everyone talking was so loud that some people decided to take their group outside, and Clara had to make sure they knew where to find them afterwards, but after about half an hour they managed to get everyone back. Solomon and Alik had agreed to write down everything people came back with. It was interesting to hear how different they were in some ways, and which things came up again and again. Here were some of the suggestions:

- To be able to smell the salty smell of the sea, with no other nasty smells in the way.
- A clean beach, with clean water where the children can play and swim safely.

- Somewhere to sit and look out over the sea and enjoy it.
- Somewhere for the children to catch crabs off the quayside.
- Somewhere for the fishermen to put their fish scraps back into the sea.
- Somewhere for the fishermen to dry and mend their nets.
- For the harbour to be an attractive place to be, so everyone can enjoy it.
- A place to be proud of, that will attract people to visit the town, the shops, and the seafront.

"Okay," said Clara, "these are our aspirations for the harbour and if we work together, I think we can make them a reality. Solomon over to you."

"So, now we know what we want our harbour to look like when it is finished," said Solomon. "We've added in the first batch of the Aspiration ingredient and Ashar has told us about the other main ingredient which is Reflection… but I think we need a dash of Alik's treasure here – Responsibility." Alik stepped forward.

"Responsibility starts with thinking about the choices you're making and the impact they will have. You have a choice now – you can go away and not bother to do the 'reflection' task that Ashar has given you, or you can choose to do it as he has asked and come back with what you discover."

There was a murmur around the hall, some people had clearly thought they could just forget about the reflection task, and no-one would notice. Solomon beckoned Clara to the front again.

"That fits with the second part of Aspiration," she said. "It's not just about coming up with ideas about what you want, it's also about putting in the effort that is needed to make them a reality."

"So," said Solomon, "to be successful at our first layer of the Harbour Cake we've got the first Aspiration ingredient in the bowl, now we need to add in Reflection, some more Aspiration and a touch of Responsibility. Here is the recipe card. Are you up for making this cake a reality?"

"Yes," came the loud response from all round the hall, people were getting into this now.

"Then we'll meet back here the day after tomorrow and hear about what happened when you did your Reflection," said Solomon. "If you aren't able to be here, tell someone who is coming what you noticed when you reflected about the harbour, and ask them to put it in the mix. That way we won't be leaving out any of the ingredients we need, and we'll get the best cake."

There was a buzz of energy around the hall as people went out. Clara noticed the Mayor go back over to the group of people he had been speaking to when they first arrived, his friends maybe. She wondered what they were saying but couldn't work out from their faces if they were happy or not.

Quite a few people came up to the team and told them how good they thought it had been, and how pleased they would be if the harbour ended up like they hoped. The team were incredibly pleased as people seemed to be getting the idea about treasures, they just hoped people would use the treasures in the way they had suggested so that the Harbour Project aspirations were achieved.

After a few minutes, the Mayor came across.

"Well, I have to admit it seems to be going alright so far," he said, not exactly apologising for his rude attitude earlier, "let's hope you can keep it up... we'll have to see what comes back in a couple of days. Remember, it won't be a success until the harbour looks like we want it to!"

"That's up to everyone, not just us!" said Clara. The challenge was on.

HARBOUR CAKE RECIPE CARD:
Layer 1 (Cake)

Treasure Ingredients

2 x Aspiration
1 x Reflection

Spoonful: *Responsibility*

Method:

1. Identify what you want to get away from or stop happening:
   - *Stop and notice what things are NOT how you want them*
   - *Identify things you want to get rid of or change?*

2. Identify exactly what you DO want things to be like in the future.

3. Take responsibility and put in the effort needed to change things.

Harbour Aspirations

We want our harbour to have:

- The lovely salty smell of the sea, with no other nasty smells
- A clean beach, with clean water, where the children can swim and play safely.
- Somewhere to sit and look out over the sea and enjoy it.
- Somewhere for the children to catch crabs off the quayside.
- Somewhere for the fishermen to put their fish scraps back into the sea.
- Somewhere for the fishermen to dry and mend their nets.

We want our harbour to be:

- An attractive place to be, so that everyone can enjoy it.
- A place to be proud of, that will attract people to visit the town, the shops, and the seafront.

Chapter 20: The Second Layer

A couple of days later when they came back together, there were slightly fewer people crowding in the hall, but that was to be expected as not everyone could spare the time. The Mayor's friends were back too, but a slightly smaller group of them. At the front of the hall Phoebe, Rocco, and Dante had put up great big sunny poster with the 'Harbour Aspirations' they'd come up with on the first day, to remind everyone of what they were aiming to achieve and a 'recipe card' ready for each layer.

They started by getting feedback from the Reflection task that Ashar had asked them to do. They were pleased to find that a lot of the people there had done it, and even brought feedback from others unable to be there. When they put it all together, it wasn't surprising that the harbour had been described as disgusting, but at least they knew a bit more about what was wrong. The two big issues were smell and mess, as they'd expected, but people had managed to notice quite a bit more detail about them:

1. The smell - people had noticed the smell was worse in the evening, especially when the tide was out, and they had managed to work out a few different smells that were part of it:
   - a rotting fish smell.
   - a smell like rotting food.
   - a smell like poo.

2. The mess - people said it was not just in the harbour itself, but in the streets around it too. The things people noticed were:
   - Rubbish and rotting food scraps on the ground.
   - Seagull poo everywhere
   - Piles of smelly fishing nets
   - Rubbish floating in the water in the harbour itself.

90

- Bits of dead fish in the water, some of which were tangled up in broken bits of net or string when the tide went out these were lying on the sand
- Mud, dung, and sand on the streets making your feet mucky, especially if there had been light rain.
- The beach itself was scattered with rubbish and bits of dead fish.

"Well done everyone," said Clara, "so far, we've used three treasures: we had the first part of Aspiration in the bowl, deciding what we want the harbour to be like, and you've added in Reflection mixed with the second part of Aspiration and a bit of Responsibility by making responsible choices and putting in the effort. As a result, we've identified exactly what problems we need to solve. We've baked the first layer of the cake. Give yourselves a cheer – it's a great start!"

Everyone gave themselves a cheer and a clap. Then Solomon stepped forward again.

"Now let's move on to the second layer, which will be an icing layer; always remembering what we are aspiring to achieve." He pointed at the poster with the aspirations on it and read them out so that even the people who couldn't read would remember them.

"For the next layer" he continued, "the main ingredients are my treasure, Reasoning, and a new part of Ashar's Reflection, but we may need a teaspoonful of a couple of other ingredients as well, so listen carefully. Everything needs to be mixed well together so let's explain what we need to put in."

There was a murmur of excitement round the hall; people seemed to be finding it quite fun to think of it like making a cake. Solomon went first.

"The part of the Reasoning treasure we are going to use is one of my favourite bits… looking for evidence. It's a bit like being a detective, searching out information and facts to work out what they are telling you." There was a murmur of interest around the room, so Solomon continued.

"You've noticed what the problems are, now we are going to become detectives and look for information and evidence to find out what is causing the problems. You can do this in a group or by yourself but choose the things that most annoyed you and see if you can work out why or how they are happening."

"Whoever's behind that dreadful smell needs to be put in jail!" someone shouted, and everyone laughed.

"Very good!" said Solomon joining in the laughter, then after waiting for it to quieten a little he added. "I'm not sure putting everyone in jail who might be contributing to this problem is going to solve much though … I'm not sure we've got a big enough jail!" More laughter.

"Maybe this is where a teaspoon of Alik's treasure, Responsibility, comes back in," Solomon added, beckoning Alik to come forward.

"Yes," said Alik, "it's true that some of the evidence might point to other people being responsible for some things, but I suspect it will also show that most people could do something to make things better…. and if we are going to solve it at all, we need to do it as a team."

Everyone knew this was true and there were a few 'hear, hears" across the room. Solomon picked it back up again.

"So, we might need a couple of days to mix this layer, but the first ingredient is Reasoning – which on this occasion means looking for evidence and information. We are going to mix it with a teaspoon of Responsibility by acting as a team, and then, very carefully mix in some more Reflection. Tell us about that Ashar."

"This time the part of the Reflection treasure we are going to use is asking questions of ourselves and others," explained Ashar, "because doing that will help us understand what is happening better."

"What do you mean asking questions of ourselves?" asked someone. "We all know detectives ask questions of other people to get information, but we don't need to ask ourselves questions … we already know the answers!" More laughter – it was great that everyone was having so much fun.

"Ah… but do we?" asked Ashar mysteriously. "I often put things down without thinking about it – then when I can't find them later, I have to ask myself 'Where did I put that?', because we often don't notice what we're doing." There was a ripple of recognition round the room. Ashar continued.

"And I sometimes I say and do mean things and upset people I care about," he admitted, "and I have to ask myself 'Why did I do that?' before I understand what was going on in my own head or notice that I feel things I hadn't realised. It's hard to change what we do, if we don't notice we are doing it, or understand why we are doing it. That is why we sometimes need to ask ourselves questions too."

"I think we'd all have to admit to doing both those things," said Solomon, feeling proud of his friend's honesty, "this layer of the cake is about understanding what is going on – what is behind the fact that the harbour is messy and smelly. We need to open our minds and our eyes to look hard for facts and evidence, but we also need to be brave enough to ask *ourselves* questions, as well as other people."

"So maybe Courage is another ingredient we need to mix in!" a young woman near the front said in a rather quiet voice.

"Exactly" said Solomon "well said! Courage is another ingredient we need to mix in – it's another treasure, and one that you clearly have!"

The young woman beamed, it was true, it had taken courage to speak up in a crowd this size and she had never done it before. Clara saw her smile, and it made tears come to her eyes, this is exactly what they had hoped for. Solomon had noticed too.

"We are not the only ones with treasures around here," Solomon continued, "and we certainly aren't the only ones who can use the treasures we have. So, are you ready to start mixing the ingredients for this layer?"

"Yes" came the enthusiastic reply.

"And don't forget" said Alik, "the more we do this as a team, the better the results will be so, the same as before – tell others and get them doing it as well, so you can bring their evidence and information back next time, if they can't be here."

"Off you go!" said Solomon and people set off out of the hall with a hum of enthusiasm for their task.

Clara noticed the Mayor had come in at the back of the hall and was once again talking to his group of friends. He hadn't been there at the start as she knew he'd been busy elsewhere, but she hadn't noticed when he'd arrived. They looked deep in discussion, but again she couldn't work out from their faces whether they were pleased or not. She wished she could be a fly on the wall of the conversation. Just then Phoebe came past, so she pulled her to one side.

"You see that group of people the Mayor is talking to," Clara whispered, "do you know who they are? Some of them look a bit familiar but I can't place them. He's always talking to them."

Phoebe glanced over discretely.

"Ah yes," she said, "it's all his rich friends. There's the owner of that big hotel down by the harbour, and that's the owner of the fish market. The Mayor likes to keep in with the people who have money and influence around here."

"You really do know everyone don't you?" said Clara, smiling at her friend.

"It's part of being Resourceful," laughed Phoebe, "if you help other people, and get to know them, they'll often help you when you need it. I guess the Mayor is resourceful too!"

"Maybe he is," said Clara, still wondering what their serious looking conversation was about. As she was looking, she noticed another gentleman standing away from the group. Just as she noticed him, he turned and saw her looking. He started to come across, beckoning her to follow him.

He led her off to one side where the Mayor couldn't see them.

"I saw you looking at the Mayor and his rich friends" he said, "he isn't being that kind to you and your friends, is he?" Clara wasn't sure how to react.

"Maybe not in some ways," she said carefully, "but he has given us this chance to prove our treasures are valuable, and to show everyone how Positive Pirates can help."

"That's true," said the man, "I wonder what's in it for him? I just want you to know his friends aren't the only ones with money, and if you are willing to help me, maybe I can help you. I'll be in touch." Then, without giving Clara a chance to ask him anymore, he turned and left.

Clara wondered what all that was about, but she soon forgot about it in all the excitement.

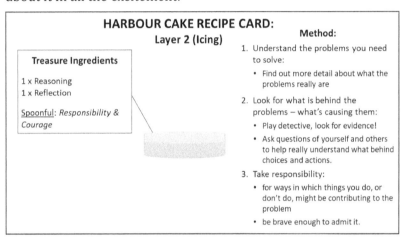

HARBOUR CAKE RECIPE CARD:

Layer 2 (Icing)

Treasure Ingredients

1 x Reasoning
1 x Reflection

Spoonful: *Responsibility & Courage*

Method:

1. Understand the problems you need to solve:
   - Find out more detail about what the problems really are
2. Look for what is behind the problems – what's causing them:
   - Play detective, look for evidence!
   - Ask questions of yourself and others to help really understand what behind choices and actions.
3. Take responsibility:
   - for ways in which things you do, or don't do, might be contributing to the problem
   - be brave enough to admit it.

Chapter 21: Getting Rid of the Bad Stuff

Two days later they were all back. The enthusiasm had spread, and the group was bigger once again. It took quite some time to hear all the evidence and information that had been discovered, but they made sure everyone got to share what they'd found. When it was all put together, this is what they'd uncovered about the causes of each problem:

The rotten fish smell: This seemed to be coming from two places – the piles of fishing nets that were all around the harbour were part of the problem, but the main source of the smell were the bits of dead fish that were floating in the water or stranded rotting on the sand. It was worse when the tide was out and on a hot day, as the sun made the fish decay more quickly when it wasn't in the water.

The rotting food smell: Sometimes it was difficult to separate this out from the smell of rotting fish, but quite a few people found scraps of left-over food that had just been dropped in the street or thrown into the harbour area. Several of the shops and pubs also threw their scraps and left-over food into their back yards, or even into the harbour, thinking the rats, seagulls or fish would eat them.

The smell of poo: As hardly any houses had flushing toilets, and farmers found poo and dung to be good fertilizer for their crops, the town had an area where people could empty buckets of poo, so that it could be taken and delivered to the local farms. Unfortunately, this area was quite near the harbour and, although it had walls around it, the smell still wafted over the harbour and shops.

The rubbish in the streets, harbour and on the beach: Some people had been exceptionally good at looking in more detail at the evidence, and they had noticed the rubbish was a mix of:

- things that were probably dropped by people coming from the nearby shops (bags, food wrappings, newspaper)
- things that looked like they had probably been dropped in the market square, including some papers that seemed to have come from the Town Hall; they had somehow found their way to the harbour, probably having been blown there by the wind.
- things that looked like they had come from boats and ships in the harbour area (bits of net, broken equipment, bits of rag).

The seagull poo: The rotting fish and scraps of food had attracted an exceptionally large number of seagulls to the harbour area, and they were not fussy about where they dropped their poo.

The bits of fish in the harbour and on the beach: These were coming from two places – the multitude of fishing boats that used the harbour, and the fish market just next to the harbour. Whether the fish was gutted and prepared on the boats, or at the market, the practice was to just throw the guts, off-cuts, and scraps into the harbour, expecting it to be washed away or eaten by crabs or other fish. However, the tide went out so slowly that unless it was a particularly high tide and a windy day, most of the fish scraps just stayed in the harbour area going rotten.

The mud, dung, and sand on the streets: Horses were used to pull most vehicles and their dung was left on the street. The wheels of the carriages they pulled also brought mud in from the country roads and, along with the feet of the people walking around, did a good job of spreading the dung, mud, and sand from the beach, all around the local area. It made for a horrible smelly mess that was only reduced, but never actually washed away, by rain, even when it was heavy.

Once they'd heard all the evidence, no-one was surprised that the harbour was a mess and smelled disgusting. Those who had asked themselves questions about how it all got there knew that everyone in the town had a part to play in it. With all the evidence recorded, Solomon summed it up.

"You've all done an excellent job of finding evidence and asking questions to work out the causes of the problems. With that layer of the icing in place, we can move on to looking at what ingredients we need for the next layer of cake, which will be about solving the problems. Clara is going to tell us about this layer."

"This is getting exciting now," said Clara. "This layer needs a good mix of quite a lot of ingredients. We still need the Reflection ingredient we used last time, to ask questions of ourselves and others, but this time we are going to add in some new things. We also need another, slightly different bit of the Reasoning ingredient, which Solomon will tell you about, but the two main ingredients this time are Responsibility, Alik's treasure, which we've only used as a seasoning before, and Phoebe's treasure, Resourcefulness. We may also need couple of spoonsful of Dante's treasure, Resilience, to help it along. Alik, can you start by telling us how we add Responsibility?"

"We've already talked about Responsibility being thinking about the choices you are making and the impact you are having," said Alik, "we need to put in a lot more now and mix it with Ashar's Reflection ingredient. Looking at the problems we need to solve we want you to ask yourselves which ones are being caused most by choices you are making." A hand shot up from the crowd and Alik invited them to speak.

"I'm a fisherman," said the man, "and it seems obvious that it is those of us who catch fish, and sell them, who are making choices to throw bits of fish into the harbour and leave our nets in piles on the harbour. So, we are responsible for the rotting fish smell, and bits of rotting fish on the beach."

"That is an excellent example of accepting responsibility sir!" said Alik happily, bowing at the fisherman. "You realise it is your choices that are causing part of the problem. Are you willing to take responsibility, for finding some different choices that will help with solving the problem?"

"Yes of course!" said the man who looked around at the other fisherfolk in the room, "I hope we're all willing to look together at how we can do that." There were nods and murmurs of agreement, from fisherfolk and fish market folk all around the room.

"There, we have a wonderful example of adding double Responsibility into the mix!" said Alik proudly, "clearly I'm not

98

the only one who has Responsibility as a treasure. The fisherfolk are going to take responsibility individually, and as a team, to look at how they can make different choices to solve some of the problems they're responsible for. Are there other teams willing to do the same?"

Lots of other hands shot up and it didn't take too long before there were several teams who were going to work together like the fisherfolk:

- The shopkeepers and pub landlords would look at their choices about rubbish and food waste.
- A group which included some farmers, the bloke with the 'poo cart' and lot of townsfolk, were going to look at the poo smell problem.
- Several other groups of townsfolk had agreed to look at theirs and others' choices about rubbish, muck on the ground and the seagull poo problems.

"Working together in your teams," said Alik, "look at the impact of the choices you and others are making. You're probably making them for a reason, even if the reason is only that it's what you've always done, or it's the easiest thing to do, but to add in Responsibility, you need to come up with ideas about other choices that you could make, that might have a better impact."

"Keep adding in a touch of Reflection" said Ashar, "by asking yourselves and each other questions, and also by noticing what does and doesn't already work, as your choices might be to do more of some things and less of others."

"Then when you have come up with some ideas, add in some Reasoning too," said Solomon. "Do this by testing out ideas you come up with by asking yourself a new question – What if? To help you think it through. Ashar – give us an idea to try this on."

"What if we put rubbish bins along the streets?" suggested Ashar to Solomon. "So people don't drop rubbish on the ground."

Solomon thought for a moment before answering.

"Well, unless someone emptied them regularly, they'd overflow and still cause rubbish in the streets!" said Solomon.

"Asking 'what if' helps you work out whether your idea will have the impact you want, or whether it might need some tweaking to solve a slightly different problem it creates."

"Now we need our other main ingredient, Resourcefulness" said Clara, "Phoebe your turn."

Phoebe bounced up with Dante next to her. "You add in Resourcefulness in three ways. Firstly, by being clear what you are trying to achieve, which in this case means remembering what our aspirations for the harbour are. Then secondly, by believing that we can achieve them and find solutions, so that we don't give up if the brilliant solution doesn't just immediately jump out at us!"

"That's where you may need a teaspoon of Resilience," said Dante. "Don't give up - stick at it and try to find different ways to look at things to see if they help."

"The third part of the Resourcefulness treasure is knowing when you need help and being willing to ask for it," said Phoebe. "There might be some things you want to change, but you can't make it happen by yourself, so you need help."

Bill, the Harbourmaster waved to get Phoebe's attention.

"I think I have an example of that, Phoebe," he said in a loud voice. "I think the fisherfolk group might struggle to find new ways to get rid of their rotting fish, and drying their nets without leaving them in piles, unless I agree to make some changes in the way the harbour works."

The fisherfolk nodded.

"That is a wonderful example, Bill," said Phoebe excitedly, "so are you willing to work with the fisherfolk group and help them with finding the best solutions to the rotting fish problems?"

"Indeed, I am," said Bill. "I'd be very happy to be responsible for helping with making things better."

"I think we will need help with the poo smell problem!" said a scruffy looking man, who it turned out was the man who ran the Night Soil 'poo cart' business. "It might cost money to move it to somewhere where it doesn't cause such problems." Clara noticed the Mayor was striding to the front of the hall, she hoped it was good news. He clomped up onto the stage while everyone waited.

"I'm sure where good solutions require some money behind them," he said sternly, "I will make every effort to find the money to make them happen - as long as they <u>are</u> good solutions mind you!"

He turned to Alik and added. "I can be Responsible too you know." Alik nodded happily. Clara was relieved, as she'd been finding it hard to work out what the Mayor really thought.

"Right, everyone, you know the teams you are working with," said Clara in her loudest voice. "I think we will need to give this layer a week to give you a chance to get together and agree your ideas. If you need advice about who might be able to help, then just come and ask us, or the Mayor, and we'll do our best to find the right person to help you. We'll see you back here in a week."

"Don't forget," said Alik, "if there are people who couldn't be here today who can help, include them in your team. The more people we have taking responsibility for achieving our harbour aspirations, the easier they will be to achieve."

"Go for it!" said the Mayor in a booming voice; it seemed that at last the Mayor was firmly on board!

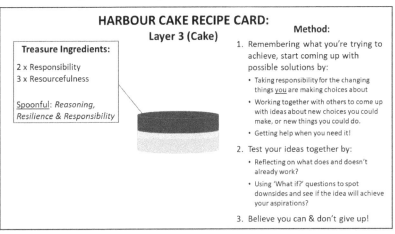

HARBOUR CAKE RECIPE CARD:
Layer 3 (Cake)

Treasure Ingredients:

2 x Responsibility
3 x Resourcefulness

Spoonful: *Reasoning, Resilience & Responsibility*

Method:

1. Remembering what you're trying to achieve, start coming up with possible solutions by:
   • Taking responsibility for the changing things <u>you</u> are making choices about
   • Working together with others to come up with ideas about new choices you could make, or new things you could do.
   • Getting help when you need it!

2. Test your ideas together by:
   • Reflecting on what does and doesn't already work?
   • Using 'What if?' questions to spot downsides and see if the idea will achieve your aspirations?

3. Believe you can & don't give up!

Chapter 22: Adding in the Good Stuff

That week was a busy one. Anyone walking around the harbour kept bumping into little groups of people thinking seriously together or having excited discussions about an idea of some kind. Even in the pubs the conversations were rather unusual, as everyone was testing out ideas about how they thought the various problems could be solved; it felt like the whole of the town was getting involved, which was lovely to see. The Positive Pirates were sought out by a number of teams wanting help with ideas or advice about how to mix their ingredients well. Even the Mayor had been kept busy.

When everyone came back to the hall a week later, to share what they'd come up with, you could feel the excitement and energy. This time the Mayor wanted to be at the front of the hall as well, not hiding at the back with his mates, but he let Clara introduce the session.

"Welcome back everyone. We know you're all very keen to tell us what ideas you've come up with for solving our problems, and we're extremely keen to hear, so that is what we will start with. Taking one problem at a time and hearing any ideas anyone has come up with for solving them."

As before it took quite some time to collect all the ideas. There was even laughter as some teams decided to share their more whacky ideas as well as the ones that they thought might really work. One of the teams who had been thinking about the problem with the smell of poo, suggested that giving every house one of those new flushing toilets would solve the problem, but everyone took this as a joke as no-one believed that would ever happen!

Once the ideas for each problem had been shared, and they had them all written up at the front, it was clear that some ideas would help with, or solve, more than one problem, which was extremely exciting. Clara got up to speak again.

"These are great ideas and together they make the 'ideas' layer of cake an incredibly good one. Now we need to use a slightly different mix of ingredients to form the next layer. The next layer is an icing layer and I think we can make it together in this hall, because it's about deciding. We need to decide which of these amazing ideas we'll put into action. They are all good ideas, but we may not need to do all of them, and we may not be able to do all of them. Solomon, tell us about what ingredients we need for this icing layer." Solomon got up.

"There are two main ingredients here and they need to be very well mixed together with a dash of a third ingredient. The two main ingredients are Reasoning and Resourcefulness, so Phoebe and I are going to show you how they mix together here." Phoebe came and stood next to Solomon.

"For each idea we need to ask a series of questions," said Solomon. "First, do we have all the information we need to know whether this will work? If the answer is 'no' then we will put the idea on one side – we can always come back to it if we need to. If the answer is 'yes' then we can move on to Phoebe's question."

"I have one question with three parts," said Phoebe, "the one question is 'What do we need to make this work?' and the first two parts of it are 'What <u>things</u> do we need' and 'What <u>people</u> do we need?' Then the last part mixes with the third ingredient – which is Alik's Responsibility." Alik came forward.

"To make some of these ideas work we might will need other people to take Responsibility," explained Alik, "as we might need them to make different choices than they have been making. Sometimes it will just be a few people, but sometimes it might be lots of people."

"So," said Phoebe, "the third part of my 'what do we need' question is, 'how do we help people to take Responsibility and make these new choices'?"

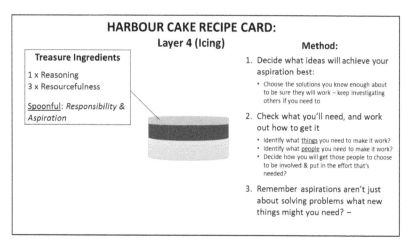

HARBOUR CAKE RECIPE CARD:
Layer 4 (Icing)

Treasure Ingredients

1 x Reasoning
3 x Resourcefulness

Spoonful: *Responsibility & Aspiration*

Method:

1. Decide what ideas will achieve your aspiration best:
   - Choose the solutions you know enough about to be sure they will work – keep investigating others if you need to

2. Check what you'll need, and work out how to get it
   - Identify what <u>things</u> you need to make it work?
   - Identify what <u>people</u> you need to make it work?
   - Decide how you will get those people to choose to be involved & put in the effort that's needed?

3. Remember aspirations aren't just about solving problems what new things might you need? –

They started with the ideas that might help with more than one problem, and then they went through every idea and tested them out as Solomon, Phoebe and Alik had described. Once this was done, these were the ideas they'd decided would solve their harbour problems best.

<u>The rotten fish smell</u>: Having looked more at the evidence it was clear that hardly any of the rotting fish smell was coming from the nets. They did look messy though, so it was agreed to put up some poles near the harbour so that the smaller boats, who couldn't dry their nets onboard, could hang their nets on them to dry, which would look nicer, and they'd dry more quickly so would smell less.

The real cause of the fish smell was all the fit bits that were tossed into the actual harbour as the tide was not strong enough to wash the fish out to sea. The smell was much worse when the tide was out, as all the rotting bits that didn't go out with the tide got stuck in the sand. It was agreed that the Harbourmaster would forbid anyone from dropping anything into the harbour itself, and some new steps and walkways would be added, to make it easier for the boats to take their fish scraps and toss them off the other side of the wall into the sea, where they would get washed away.

<u>Rubbish and rotting food in the streets</u>: Everyone knew that reducing the amount of food scraps lying around would also help with the seagull poo problem as the seagulls were attracted by

the food. There would always be seagulls, and it wasn't possible to put nappies on them to stop them pooing, but if there were fewer birds, or they were less well fed, it could reduce the problem.

Aside from the seagulls, everyone agreed there were two solutions to the rubbish problem:

- Everyone in the town, and the shops, needed to stop dropping litter or throwing it into the streets. Even if they weren't dropping it in the harbour area, the wind often blew it there. This meant everyone needed to make different choices about what they did with their rubbish. It would be helped by the second, grander idea, which would cost money, but would be cheaper if everyone helped out by making different choices about their own rubbish.

- The Mayor would set up a system in the town for removing and managing rubbish and waste. It was a problem all over town so a system would be set up where the streets would be swept, and rubbish removed twice a week. A 'Dust yard' would be created along the coast just out of town where rubbish would be disposed of and re-cycled. Businesses would be expected to pay to have their rubbish taken away and households could do the same, although the poorer households could put their rubbish in the street cleaning carts and it would be taken to the Dust yard.

  ◊ The Landowner who had volunteered the land for the Dust Yard, was also interested in using some of the waste to make compost for the farmers and even selling any rubbish that could be re-used, so he hoped to make some money from that which would mean it would cost less for the town.

  ◊ There was even an idea that the fish waste from the fish market, could also be taken there, as it could make good fertilizer if mixed with other things.

◊ The Night Soil business could also put the waste into this so that it didn't have to stay long in the town.

The Poo Smell:

Everyone had identified that having the poo collection place near the harbour was causing a problem, but wherever it was it would be smelly, as great piles of poo always were. The groups working on this had come up with the idea of some clever 'poo boxes' that could be carried on the poo-carts and they had lids so that once the poo was in them the smell didn't get out.

These could then be stacked in the poo collection point until the larger horse-drawn carts could take them to the new Dust Yard to be made into fertilizer. This made the poo collection points much less smelly, so people were happier about having a few more of them round the edges of town to make collection easier. Someone also came up with the great idea that the horse poo, which was often left in the streets, could be picked up by the street cleaners and put into the poo collection points too.

"These ideas can really make a difference to our problem!" said the Mayor proudly. "I must admit I'm very surprised and impressed by how well you have all done." Everyone cheered.

"That isn't the end I'm afraid," said Clara. "It's one thing having good ideas, but the cake isn't finished until the harbour looks like we wanted it to at the start." She pointed to the aspirations they had come up with. "Before we finish this icing layer, we need to re-visit Aspiration. Will doing these things achieve all those aspirations?"

"We won't have somewhere to sit and look out over the harbour," said one voice. "We need seats!"

"... and although the streets will be cleaned twice a week, they could get quite messy in between," said another. "Maybe we need some rubbish bins!"

"... and it's all very well stopping more rubbish going into the harbour." said another, "but there's a lot of stuff in there already that isn't just going to magically vanish!"

"Well said everyone," said Clara beaming. "You've come up with some excellent ideas, but you're right, there's certainly more that needs to be done to achieve our aspirations, even when we've solved the problems – it's also about deciding what new things you want to add in - like seats and rubbish bins. What other ideas do you have about that, looking at the aspirations?"

There was a buzz of conversation around the room, and it didn't take long to come up with a list that the Mayor agreed to take away and be responsible for.

"Now onto the last cake layer," said Clara. "It will form the top of the cake and when it's done it will only be the decorations that are needed. You've all done really well on the other layers, but this one may be the hardest and take the longest." There was silence around the room. Everyone was waiting to hear what it was. "It's the action layer. Are you up for it?" A loud cheer showed they were.

"We've already talked about the first main ingredient for this layer," Clara continued. "It is Aspiration, but mixed, as before, with Responsibility and another ingredient. Aspiration isn't just about having bright ideas about what you want the future to be like, it's also about putting in the effort to do the things you need to do to make your aspiration come true. Responsibility to help each other is also mixed in with the other main ingredient we need for this layer - Dante – over to you."

"My ingredient is Resilience," said Dante. "Making your ideas into reality can be hard work and sometimes things get in the way, and it seems like you won't make it. Resilience is about sticking at things, even when they are hard. Sometimes you feel bad, and it seems too hard... you might even need to tell someone how hard it is, and that's good, as then you can encourage each other, but you keep going. Can you keep going with this last action layer?"

Once again there was a loud cheer – it was clear they were ready. Even if it meant going into the harbour and dragging all the mess out of the water, they were up for it.

"I think your job is done and it's time I took this over now," said the Mayor. "I'll admit that I didn't think you could do it, but you have shown is what sharing treasure means and I know we are going to have the best harbour around! Thank you, Positive Pirates!" Everyone cheered again.

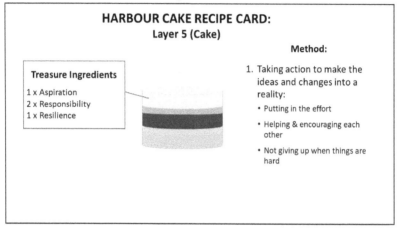

HARBOUR CAKE RECIPE CARD:
Layer 5 (Cake)

Treasure Ingredients

1 x Aspiration
2 x Responsibility
1 x Resilience

Method:

1. Taking action to make the ideas and changes into a reality:
   - Putting in the effort
   - Helping & encouraging each other
   - Not giving up when things are hard

Chapter 23: Secrets

Early the next day, Clara took her usual walk along the top of the cliff to get her thoughts together. Now the Mayor had taken over the Harbour Project she needed to go back to thinking about how she would get the money for the ship's repairs. She was very aware that if she didn't succeed this may have been the Positive Pirates one and only mission, and they would never get to sail the seas at all. That was not an option as far as she was concerned ... there had to be a way to get the money!

In the distance she could see a man walking towards her, and something about him made her think of the mysterious gentleman at the Town Hall that day, suggesting that he could help them if they helped him. She had no idea who he was, or what he wanted, but maybe he could help.

As the man came closer, she realised it was the very same gentleman. It was rather early for most people to be out, so she suspected it was no coincidence he was here and heading straight for her.

"Lovely morning!" he said, raising his hat. "I hoped I might find you here, Clara."

"Yes, it is a beautiful morning," agreed Clara, "perhaps though, it might be polite if you told me your name, as you clearly know mine, and even where I go for walks!" The man chuckled politely.

"Ah yes," he said, "apologies for the cloak and dagger approach the other day. I had my reasons, and I didn't want our friend the Mayor to see me talking to you just yet. My name is Samuel Hissey – at your service." As he said this, he took his hat off again and bowed to Clara very dramatically.

Clara wasn't sure she entirely trusted Samuel Hissey, and she wondered why he hadn't wanted the Mayor to see him talking to her. The way he had said 'our friend' about the Mayor suggested he was anything but a friend. She decided to be straight with him.

"Thank you, it's good to know your name, but I'm afraid I don't know who you are," she said, "and I'm not sure why you wouldn't want the Mayor to see us talking. You said something about us helping each other – perhaps you could explain clearly what you were talking about."

"Ah yes," said Mr Hissey again. "Well, let's just say I have reasons why I don't want the Mayor to know about this just yet. As for explaining myself, I think it is enough to say that I can see the value in what you and your team have to offer, and I understand you need money to repair your ship. Let's just say that the Mayor isn't the only one with wealthy friends and, if the conditions are right, I would like to get you the money you need."

"That sounds very kind," said Clara, "but of course I have to ask what you mean by 'If the conditions are right' – what conditions are you talking about?" Clara knew they really needed the money, but something inside her wasn't comfortable and she wasn't sure why.

"The only condition I require is complete secrecy," he said as if it was nothing at all to ask. "If we make an agreement, then I will get you all the money you need, but I will be the one to decide when and how anyone else gets to know about it. It will just be between you and me."

"You mean you're asking me not to even tell the rest of my crew?" asked Clara, not liking this at all.

"I don't think that is too much to expect considering how much money we'll be talking about," said Mr Hissey. "I've told you I have my reasons, and I expect you to trust me and take me at my word."

"You may not think it's a lot to ask," said Clara, feeling less and less comfortable with this, "but that's not the way I work with my team. How long would I have to keep this secret for?"

"Until I tell you otherwise!" clarified Mr Hissey. "I won't keep you waiting too long, but the timing has to be right and only I can make that judgement. If you want the money, then you will have to change the way you do things and keep the secret."

"I need some time to think about it," said Clara. She knew how much they needed the money, but somehow keeping this a secret didn't feel wise.

"Then I will meet you here tomorrow at the same time," said Mr Hissey, "but make sure you come alone, and remember, secrecy or no money. It's quite simple. Good day." He nodded his head slightly, then walked off as if he had not a care in the world.

Clara wondered what to do as she walked back home. She was due to meet the team soon to talk about what next and she didn't like to keep secrets from them, but on the other hand, if their Positive Pirate aspiration was going to have any hope of coming true, they did need the money.

She didn't want to lose this wonderful opportunity, nor did she want to let her team down; maybe if they could think of another way to get the money then she could tell Mr Samuel Hissey he could take his secrets and go away!

An hour later when the team came together, Clara wasn't quite as cheerful as she might have been after their harbour success, but she'd decided to try and forget about him for a while and see if they could find a solution by themselves.

Rocco was back with the team again. He'd tried to stay in the background for the Harbour Project because he wasn't sure the Mayor was that keen on actual pirates, and he wanted to spend some time on his old ship before leaving. However, he had been there at the end of the last session and had seen everyone's enthusiasm, so he knew their plan had been a success. Clearly everyone had got the idea about what Positive Pirate treasures were and how using them could make the world, or rather the harbour, better, but Clara and the team didn't seem quite as full of beans as he'd expected. He had an idea why.

"I can see why you aren't pleased," he said, "that was a pretty mean trick the Mayor pulled yesterday!" The others looked puzzled.

111

"What do you mean Rocco?" asked Solomon. It was Rocco's turn to look puzzled.

"Well, you'd put in all that hard work," explained Rocco, starting to think he might have got it wrong, "and the Mayor just took it over at the point where it was starting to be a success!"

"Oh, I see what you mean," said Clara. "It's true it does feel a bit weird not being so involved at the most difficult bit, but we did say we weren't going to do it all and they know what they need to do – now they need to do it. I don't think it was a trick or meant to be mean."

"In fact," said Alik, "I think the Mayor has it exactly right, he's taking responsibility for it now, along with the others, and, as he said, we've done our bit!"

"Yes," agreed Phoebe, "we have achieved what we wanted out of it, I think they all understand what we mean by sharing treasures and even how to use treasures to make things better. Whether they actually make the harbour better is up to them, and it has always been the Mayor who most wanted to make that happen."

"Still," said Ashar, "I must admit I'm really pleased about that, but it does feel a bit of an anti-climax now we're not involved – I quite enjoyed the challenge of doing something together and working out how to share our treasures. It was fun." The others all agreed.

"I guess it doesn't mean we can't help just like everyone else," said Dante, "unless you have other plans Clara?"

"That's a good question," said Clara. "I'm sure you're right Dante, that the Mayor isn't going to turn down any other help we can offer along the way, but in terms of what else we have to do; we aren't any further forward with our big problem. We still don't have enough money to do the repairs on the ship, and without them we aren't going anywhere."

"We can still use the naming ceremony to get people to give us stuff we can use for the ship," said Phoebe, trying to be positive.

"Hopefully, the harbour will be finished by then so I'm sure people will be keen to help," said Dante. "We might get what we need then mightn't we?"

"Maybe," said Clara, wondering if she should say something. "I do want us to do some thinking about how we want to adapt the ship as well, I've got lots of plans, but we need actual money to get the repairs done first, otherwise there's no point."

"There must be a way," said Phoebe, "we've just got to find it!"

There was silence while everyone tried to think of ideas but, seeing their faces Clara could see no-one had any. She couldn't bear it.

"There might be a way," she said quietly, almost to herself, "but I'm not sure it's the right thing to do."

"Ooh," said Phoebe excitedly, not picking up on Clara's uncertainty, "I knew there would be, tell us more!"

"I'm afraid I can't," said Clara, "because if I do, it won't work."

"You mean it might jinx it if you tell us?" asked Rocco, who was used to pirates thinking that way. "I must admit I didn't have you down as the superstitious type!"

"It's not that," said Clara, wishing she hadn't said anything, "I've already said too much. Forget I said anything... just keep thinking of any ideas you can come up with... please."

Ashar and Dante looked at each other; Clara was not her usual self and clearly something was wrong.

"You do know you can talk to us if you're worried about something," said Dante, "you don't have to sort it out by yourself."

"I'm afraid on this occasion I do," said Clara, "and I'd love to tell you, but I can't. Please forget it."

"If something inside you is telling you something isn't right," said Ashar, "then you need to listen. Maybe there's someone else you trust that you can talk to, if you can't talk to us, because it sounds like you need to talk to someone."

"Thanks, Ashar," said Clara, glad someone understood. "I know you're right. It's just tricky."

"Take your time" said Ashar, "I'm sure you'll know what to do."

"Thanks," said Clara. "Perhaps I'll go for a walk and have a think. Don't worry, but if anyone has any ideas how to get the money then now's a good time to come up with them. I'll see you in a while."

The team watched her go, wishing they could help but having no real clue what the problem was.

Chapter 24: What's Important?

Clara knew Ashar was right, she needed to talk to someone, and it had to be today as Mr Hissey would be expecting an answer tomorrow morning. She set off to have another walk along the cliffs, but as she walked around the house, she was so lost in her thoughts that she didn't see Mary, who was crouched down doing some gardening, and almost tripped over her.

"Oops. Hi love," Mary said, getting up from her weeding, "you looked like you had the world on your shoulders for a moment there. Are you okay?"

"Not really," said Clara honestly, "but I'm not allowed to tell anyone why!"

"Who said so?" asked Mary, "seems to me it's up to you if you want to tell anyone when something's bothering you, not anyone else."

Clara smiled. Mary had a lovely way of looking at things, a bit like Dante. As she smiled, all of a sudden Clara knew that Mary was right. No-one else had the right to tell her not to talk to someone she trusted when she needed to, and certainly not Mr Hissey, when he was the one putting her in a difficult position in the first place. She also knew the person she wanted to talk to was Mary as, whatever the problem, Mary would listen and give calm and sensible advice.

"Thank you," said Clara, "that helps, and I would really like to talk to you about something, but it's supposed to be a secret, so please don't tell anyone." Mary smiled at her.

"How about I join you for your walk and you tell me what's bothering you. Then you and I can decide between us if it needs to be a secret or not" she suggested. "You know you can trust me never to do anything to hurt you don't you?"

"Yes, I know I can trust you," said Clara, feeling relieved. "I was going for a walk, but actually can we go inside where it's more private, as I don't want anyone to see me talking at the moment."

They went into the house and Mary made a pot of tea, while Clara told her all about her two encounters with Mr Hissey, and what he had said. Mary listened carefully.

"I know Mr Hissey says he has his reasons to keep this secret," Clara finished, "and he wants me to just trust him, but something doesn't feel right. Ashar says I must listen to that feeling, but it's just a feeling, and if I blow this and we don't get that money then I'll be letting everyone down."

"I know how important getting the money for repairs is for you and the team," said Mary, "but I know your team care about you, so do you really think they would want you to do something that doesn't feel right, just to get the money?"

"No, I suppose not," admitted Clara. "I just don't want to let them down. Maybe he does have a good reason for wanting it to be a secret, but I can't think of one, and all this talk of secrets is making it hard for me to trust him."

"He's asking you to trust him, but to behave as if you don't trust your team," said Mary. "I suppose if you look at it a different way – Mr Hissey is making his choices about how he wants to do this, but it's your choice how you want to behave and what's important to you."

"Now you sound like Alik," laughed Clara, "you're right though, I guess this is an opportunity for me to choose what I aspire to be like. Is having the money more important than behaving in a way I feel comfortable with, and listening to what my quiet voice is saying to me, which is not to trust him?"

"So, what would your answer to that question be?" asked Mary.

"No – the money isn't more important," said Clara, suddenly sure. "I don't aspire to be someone who keeps secrets from my team without good reason, and the money is not more important than doing what I feel is right. If my quiet voice is right, and there is something untrustworthy about Mr Hissey, then I don't want to take his money anyway, and I won't find out whether he is untrustworthy unless I talk to other people about it. Thank you, Mary – I need to go and talk to my team."

She gave Mary a big hug and ran off back to the others, once again full of energy.

As soon as Clara had told the team about what had happened with Mr Hissey, she realised she'd made the right choice. Unlike Clara, Phoebe and Solomon had both heard of him before.

"I think your quiet voice was giving you good advice," said Phoebe. "I've come across him before. He can be very charming, but I wouldn't trust him. He was born here, but he's only just recently returned, and the rich people he says he knows aren't nice people, in fact several of them are slave traders and he has ideas about developing our harbour into a port, so he can open it up to them."

"That's what I've heard too," said Solomon. "My parents told me; they don't like him at all. I haven't met him, mind you, as he never comes into our pub because black people run it. Apparently, he's happy for us to serve him, but not to have black people in charge. I reckon he thinks we have no value except as slaves! I also hear he wants to run for Mayor as he knows our Mayor would never allow his plans, nor would Bill, if he had any choice in the matter."

"I can see why he didn't want me to talk to anyone, even you or Bill!" said Clara, "I guess he knew you'd tell me the truth about him. What puzzles me though is why he wants to give us money anyway - what he wants doesn't seem to fit with Positive Pirates at all!"

"Did you say he wanted to choose when people got told who had paid for the repairs?" asked Ashar.

"Yes," said Clara, "he was very clear about that. He would choose when. Why do you ask?"

"I've noticed before that people who want to be liked, sometimes try to link themselves to other people and things that are popular," explained Ashar. "I suspect he saw how successful our Harbour Project was, and how much people liked us, so he wanted to make himself look good by supporting us. Then he thought people might be more likely to support him."

"I bet he wanted to announce it at the naming ceremony," said Phoebe. "He's the Mayor's main rival and I guess he knows we'd expect the Mayor to name the ship. It would make the Mayor look really silly and embarrass him if he were naming a ship that it turned out his rival had paid for!"

"I think I might just go and give him a punch in the face!" said Rocco, angry at how this man was trying to use his friends.

"I know how you feel," said Dante, "but I'm sure he's convinced himself he is doing the right thing, and I'm not sure punching him will do any good. I suspect then he'll just think we're ruffians but standing up to him and telling him why we won't take his money might give him pause for thought!"

"Then that is what we will do!" said Clara.

"Well done for choosing to tell us," Alik told Clara, "it must have been hard when it meant losing the money, but it was the best thing to do."

"Thanks," said Clara, "In a way he's done me a favour, he gave me an opportunity to decide who I want to be, and I'm glad. I won't fall for that again! It's a shame about the money though."

"We'll find it" said Phoebe, "you'll see!"

Chapter 25: The Money Problem

The next morning Clara set out for her clifftop meeting with Samuel Hissey. The team had wanted to go with her, but she'd said no. She wanted to talk to him, and she knew it was likely he'd just walk off and avoid her if he saw she had brought the others, as it would be obvious that she'd told them.

The team respected her decision, but they were a bit worried about her as none of them trusted Samuel Hissey. Rocco offered to hide in a bush and jump out, but no-one wanted this to end up in a punch-up. Eventually it was agreed that Solomon and Phoebe would just happen to be going for a walk together not too far behind, so they could join Clara if she looked like she needed them. Clara agreed, but she was confident she could handle Mr Hissey now that she'd made her decision.

It didn't take long in the end. He smiled as he approached her, but somehow it wasn't a friendly smile, more a smile of someone who thinks they are about to get their way.

"Good morning," he said, raising his hat very slightly in greeting. "I trust you've made your decision?"

"I have," said Clara.

"Well, I'm sure you won't regret it," he said, assuming her answer would be 'yes', "it's the obvious choice after all – you need the money and I'm willing to get it for you!"

"I'm sure I won't regret it either," said Clara, "but I won't be taking your money. However obvious you think that choice is, it isn't the right one for us." Clara saw a look of shock cross his face, but it very quickly changed to a sort of sneer.

"I see," he said, taking on a very superior tone. "Not such a Positive Pirate after all I suspect. Would I be right in thinking you broke your promise, and shared our little secret?"

Clara was ready for that – she'd thought about exactly what she wanted to say to him.

"If you had paid any attention to our conversations," she started, "rather than just to what you wanted to say, you might have noticed that I never made you a promise about anything. You told me to keep secrets to get you to give us money, but I never agreed to do that – I've made no promises and so I've broken no promises." Mr Hissey looked at her, trying to work her out.

"I know you need the money so what has changed?" he said. "Has someone else come up with it?"

"No," said Clara, "we still need the money but, on reflection, I've decided that other things are more important. It's true I have talked to my team, and I found out a bit more about you. I have reason to believe that the money you would give us would be coming from activities that we do not approve of and would not want to support. We are not the kind of pirates who see ill-gotten gains as treasure!"

"Why should that matter?" he almost spat the question at her. "You could have used the money to get what you want – that's all I'm doing... that's what everyone does!"

"Not everyone!" said Clara. "We don't want to give anyone any reason to think we would support slavery, and taking money made from it would give that message. That is reason enough to refuse your offer, but even if that wasn't where the money was from, there is another reason to say no."

"What reason is that?" he asked, agitated, and forgetting to put on his superior tone for a moment.

"It was clear from our conversations that all you were bothered about, was whatever mysterious things you thought you would get out of giving us the money," explained Clara. "You didn't care one bit about what was best for us, or what was really important to us."

"Whatever gave you that idea?" he asked, not denying that it was true.

"Because the secrets you asked me to keep were to protect you and what you wanted to achieve, not me, or my team," said Clara. "You wanted me to trust you, but you weren't willing to trust me or my team enough to tell us the truth about why you were giving us the money, so that we could make a decision that was right for us."

"I knew you wouldn't agree if I told you!" he admitted angrily.

"You were trying to make it sound like you wanted to help us, but in fact you were trying to trick us to get what you wanted. That is not okay," said Clara. "We want to use our treasures to make life better for everyone, but you were only thinking of yourself." Samuel Hissey was lost for words.

"Having said that," said Clara, "I have learned things from this, and I hope you will too, so maybe it will make us both better people. Good day." With that she turned and walked back towards Solomon and Phoebe who had been lurking a distance behind trying not to be conspicuous but failing. Samuel Hissey watched her go, for the first time realising maybe he wasn't as clever as he thought he was.

When Clara, Solomon and Phoebe arrived back at the ship the whole team wanted to hear what had happened. They congratulated Clara on handling it well, and everyone knew they'd made the right decision, but the money problem hadn't gone away.

"We still need to find that money to get those repairs done," sighed Clara, "I don't suppose anyone has come up with any ideas, have you?"

"Maybe that's something I can help with," said a voice behind them. They all turned to see the Mayor standing at the door with Bill.

"I knew you'd come through!" beamed Phoebe, "you said if we helped you, you'd help us."

The Mayor laughed. "I actually said I would see if I could help you," he said, correcting Phoebe, "but you're right, I have 'come through' as you put it!"

"That is wonderful news," said Clara, "but what do you mean exactly?"

"That group at the back of the hall you saw me talking to," explained the Mayor, "were a group of wealthy townsfolk who I knew had the money to help you if they chose to. Like me, they weren't sure your idea was worth giving money to at first. All this talk of pirates and making the world a better place, sounded a bit far-fetched and they weren't afraid to say it. So, I challenged them to come along and see."

"Ah," said Solomon, "Is that why you were so rude about what we were trying to do? Were you overplaying the idea you agreed with them, to get them to come along?"

"Yes, sorry about that," said the Mayor slightly uncomfortably, glancing at Bill who he knew had not approved. "However, with the excellent job you did helping us to get everyone willing to change things at our harbour, they have also 'come through' as you put it. They've agreed to give you the money to pay for all the major repairs on your ship, no strings attached."

There was a stunned silence for a moment as everyone took this news in, until Rocco couldn't contain himself any longer and he shouted 'Yippee!" at the top of his voice and everyone joined him in their own version of a celebration. The Mayor put up his hand to quieten things.

"That is one of the reasons I said I would take on the harbour project from now on," he said, "we know what needs to be done and you will need to start focusing on sorting out those repairs. They are only paying for the repairs mind you, if you want any other adaptations you will have to do them yourselves, although I suspect once the harbour is finished there may be townsfolk who might be willing to help you with those."

"Understood," said Clara. "How can we thank you for this – it is excellent news?"

"You can let me be the one to break the bottle and name your ship!" said the Mayor. "But I want us to wait until your repairs are done and the harbour is finished, before we start planning the naming ceremony. I want the first big event at our new harbour to be a celebration of the Harbour Project, and I want you involved, so your naming ceremony will have to come after that."

"I could make an actual Harbour Cake if you like," offered Solomon.

"You want to say yes to that," said Phoebe, "he makes the most delicious cakes, we can tell you!"

"So, I hear," said the Mayor, "yes please!" Then he turned to Clara. "I hope the harbour work and the repairs won't take too many weeks, so you won't have to wait that long. Do we have a deal?"

Clara looked around at the others.

"We're a team," she said, "so it isn't just my decision. What do you think everyone?"

"I think it's a great idea," said Ashar, "but I think we ought to use the Harbour Project celebration to do the one last layer on the cake, the icing on the top if you like."

"What sort of icing are you thinking of?" asked the Mayor.

"Dante and I have been talking about this," said Ashar glancing at Dante who nodded, "we think its ingredients are Reflection and Resilience. Reflecting is always important when you finish something as it's a time to look back and learn from what you did."

"Yes," said Dante, "and part of Resilience is looking back and remembering the challenges you have overcome so you know you can do it again. That's especially true when you've bounced back from being in a bad situation, and the state of our harbour is definitely a bad situation!"

"I would put a bid in for Responsibility being in the mix as well," said Alik, "because keeping the harbour nice will be about everyone continuing to make good choices about what they do. It isn't just a one-off choice to make it nice."

"That sounds like a very tasty mix," said the Mayor, who was well into the Harbour Cake idea by now. "Yes, let's build in an icing layer into our celebration. So, are you happy with my proposal?"

Clara looked around at her team and they were all nodding. Their problem was solved, and they were getting the repairs done, which meant the next chapter in the Positive Pirate story could really happen; it was one that they were all very much looking forward to.

"I think it's very clear the answer is yes!" Clara said to the Mayor. "With your help in getting the repairs done, we can start to think about the future, and what better way to celebrate the start of something new for us, and Waterside harbour, than a nicely iced piece of Harbour Cake!"

"A good cause for celebration indeed!" said the Mayor.

Chapter 26: Coming Clean

The next few weeks were extremely busy in lots of ways.

The Mayor introduced the team to all the people who had agreed to put money into the ship repairs. They were all very respectable people who were now enthusiastically behind the idea of Positive Pirates. After doing several tours to show them around the ship, eventually some shipwrights were appointed and the serious business of looking at the best way to do the repairs was started.

Meanwhile the work to improve the harbour got going quite quickly as everyone was keen to make progress with it, so, with that and the ship repairs, the team certainly weren't short of things to do.

Whilst all this was going on, Solomon was busy designing what the actual Harbour Cake was going to be like. It needed to have three cake layers and three icing layers to match the number of layers they'd had in the Harbour project, and each layer needed to have a slightly different flavour or colour, to represent the different mix of ingredients each time. He knew the townsfolk wouldn't know about the final icing on the cake until the day of the celebration, but that made it even more fun.

The Mayor had agreed to provide all the ingredients needed for the Harbour Cake, but he had sworn Solomon to secrecy about exactly what was in the cake and what it would look like; he wanted it to be a nice surprise for everyone, even the Positive Pirate team. He'd given Solomon use of the large kitchen in the Town Hall to bake it and the planning was going well, but Solomon knew he needed some help from his friends.

"I'm not supposed to tell anyone what's in the cake or what it's going to be like," he told the team, "so don't even try to get that out of me, but there is something I would like your ideas about."

"How can we help you if you can't tell us stuff?" complained Phoebe. "I think we've had enough of secrets!"

"I think secrets are okay if they are just about wanting to give people a surprise they'll like," said Clara. "Is it the decoration on the top Solomon? I'm sure we can come up with some designs."

"No, sorry," said Solomon, "the Mayor had ideas about that too I'm afraid. This seems really important to him. My problem is, he wants one great big cake so that it looks spectacular, which I hope it will, but however big it is, I'm not sure there'll be enough for everyone to have some and that seems important to me, since everyone has been involved in this."

"What do you want to do?" asked Ashar, knowing his friend usually had his own ideas about things.

"Well," said Solomon, "I'm happy to make a big one, but I'd really like to make a tiny cake version as well, a simpler one, so that everyone could have one to take away, or eat on the day."

"I think that's a great idea," said Alik, "it means people could also bake their own Harbour Cakes in the future, to remember the work we all did together. They won't be as good as you at making huge cakes, but they could make little ones!"

"Even the shops could sell them!" added Phoebe. "I think the Mayor would love that idea!

"Yes, maybe he would," said Solomon thoughtfully, "I wasn't sure how to sell the idea to him, but that could work. It's just that I need to come up with a design. They can't be as complicated as the big one – he's practically got me re-building the harbour in cake at the moment!"

"Careful," warned Dante laughing, "don't go giving the game away! It's a secret remember."

"I 've told you nothing you couldn't guess," laughed Solomon, "but seriously, if we do that, I probably need to ask him to let you all into the secret anyway; I'm not sure I can do all this in time by myself."

"You know we'll be incredibly happy to help in any way we can," said Clara, "and we love coming up with ideas, but you're right, you'd better ask the Mayor first. It's nice he wants it to be a surprise, but this is a job for a team!"

"I agree," said Alik, "if he's providing the ingredients, he needs to agree to the little cakes, but then we did the Harbour Project as a team, and we should do this together too. I'm sure he'll agree."

"In the meantime, we can work on some ideas about what the little cakes could be like," said Phoebe, "and Dante can draw them up for us" Dante nodded happily.

"I'm in, especially if it means we get to help out with the baking," added Rocco. "I love cake mix!"

"The idea is that you bake it, not eat it!" laughed Solomon, but they all knew there would be at least the chance to scrape out some very large bowls.

As anticipated, the Mayor loved the little cakes idea and happily agreed for it to be a team effort. He just wanted the cake to be a special surprise and thank you to all the townsfolk who had helped out. He even agreed that Rocco was allowed to help too, which brought a big smile to his face. It didn't take them long to come up with a design for the little cakes and they got to work making lists of ingredients.

The work on the harbour took several weeks and practically everyone in the town took part in some way. The message got around about the new choices everyone needed to make, to no longer drop litter and food, and a lot of people got busy behind the scenes to put everything in place.

The new Dust Yard was set up on some land just outside town and the coopers started making lots of special boxes for transporting the muck and poo; the changes were made to the harbour and every new boat that came in was shown how and where they could get rid of their fish bits outside the harbour area.

This was all a lot of work, but the biggest event was the 'muck clearing weekend' that was arranged just two weeks before the celebration, when almost everything else was in place.

That weekend, everyone in the town, young and old, including all the Positive Pirate team, turned up in their oldest clothes and got stuck in cleaning up the harbour. It meant scraping muck from the streets, wading into the water to collect rubbish and, when the tide was out, picking up all the bits of rotting fish and food that were creating all the smell. Everyone was stinky by the end and needed to go and swim in the sea outside the harbour when the job was finished, to wash off. The next day everything was washed down so that nice new bins and seats could be put in place.

As the week of the Harbour Project celebration dawned the harbour was clean; the smell and muck were gone, and the last few finishing touches were just being put into place. The repairs on the ship were also at last fully underway, but the team were holed up in the Town Hall kitchen baking like they had never baked before.

Chapter 27: The Icing on the Cake

The Saturday of the Harbour Project celebration was a glorious one. The sun came up early, but the team was up even earlier. They hot footed it straight to the kitchen at the Town Hall to put the finishing touches to their wonderful Harbour Cake surprise.

The celebration was planned to start down at the harbour, which had been adorned with flowers. The Mayor had organised a band to be there all morning to play some cheerful tunes, so everyone could gather and have a bit of a dance if they wanted to. Then the band would lead a procession back up to the Town Hall for the final celebration.

The Mayor had also decorated the Town Hall. He'd asked all the local artists, including Dante, to do paintings and drawings of the wonderful new harbour, and all the other changes they had made, even the new Dust Yard and the Poo collection points! The pictures had been put up all around the Hall along with a number of colourful sails, which were draped from the ceiling, and it had all been finished off with more beautiful flowers, so it smelled nice too – just like the new harbour!

The idea was that they'd gather there and have the final 'icing on the cake' discussion, led by the team, before the Mayor's last surprise was revealed; it was just billed as the Mayor's 'Thank you' and most people thought it was just going to be a speech. Everyone knew the Mayor liked giving speeches!

Everything went to plan. As the band led the dancing townsfolk into the Hall it was clear there was hardly enough space for everyone, but once the band had gone to the upper balcony to make room, somehow, they managed to cram them all in.

The Mayor welcomed everyone cheerfully, saying how proud he was of what they'd managed to achieve, then handed over to

Clara to introduce the ingredients for the final layer of Harbour Cake.

"We want to start by thanking you all for baking the Harbour Cake with us, "Clara started. "We've really enjoyed sharing our treasures as the ingredients, but you've been the ones to use them and make your wonderful harbour aspirations become a reality. We have a lot to celebrate. However, the harbour may be finished, but the cake still needs its final layer – the icing on the top!" Everyone cheered. Clara waited for the cheers to subside, then she continued.

"On many cakes it is traditional to put a cherry on the top – but this is a Harbour Cake – so we felt the right thing to put on the top was a wave!" There were interested murmurs all around the room.

"I've lived on or by the sea all my life," continued Clara. "I find the sound of waves breaking on the seashore very calming, but have you ever looked at how waves that constantly break onto the beach are formed? A wave forms when some water from the previous wave slides backwards into the sea and meets up with the new water which is heading forwards towards the beach. As the retreating water slides underneath the water pushing forward, the water on top curls around it and pushes some of it back to form the crest of the wave. It is the crest that then breaks onto the shore with that wonderful swooshing sound." She showed them the process with her hands.

"So," she continued, "the wave of icing we are going to have on the top of our cake, is going to have that mix. We'll start with a treasure ingredient that helps us look backwards... and then we will use three to look forward - between them they will make our wave. Ashar, can you start us off with Reflection?" Ashar came to the front to cheers from the crowd.

"We looked forward when we made our Aspirations," started Ashar, "and now we can look back and see that we've achieved them; that's why we're here celebrating! However, that's not the only way Reflecting can help us in this final layer of the cake. To make our wave on the top we're going to stop and look back over what we've done and reflect about how each of our treasure ingredients has helped us, because it hasn't all been easy. We've written each of the treasure ingredients you've used, and for each we want you to reflect on what we've done together and decide two things:

1. What wasn't working well before you started using this treasure?
2. What was it about this treasure that worked well for you?"

The noise in the hall became very loud as everyone started talking enthusiastically. When they'd had had enough time, Ashar went through each of the treasure ingredients and asked what people had come up with, and the others wrote them down. Then they chose which were the favourites for each, by seeing which ones got the loudest cheer when they read them out. Everyone was in the mood for cheering. These were the ideas that got the biggest cheer for each:

Aspiration:

- What wasn't working was just looking at the problem – how disgusting the harbour was – that just made everyone depressed!
- What worked well was picturing what they wanted the harbour to be like – that gave everyone the energy to make it happen.

Resourcefulness:

- What didn't work was when groups, or individuals, thought they had all the answers and didn't need help.
- What worked well was realising when they needed help and finding the best person to ask for it.

Responsibility:

- What didn't work was making choices and doing things without thinking about what effect they were having (like dropping litter and not realising it ended up in the harbour).
- What worked well was working together as a team – everyone was amazed by what a difference they'd all made when they worked together!

Reasoning:

- What didn't work well was assuming the first idea you came up with was always the best one.
- What did work well was playing detective and looking for evidence and using 'what if' questions to explore whether ideas would work.

Reflection:

- What didn't work well was rushing into things without stopping and thinking.
- What did work well was asking questions of yourself and others to make sure you really understood what was happening.

Resilience:

- What didn't work well was expecting things to be easy and getting upset when they weren't.
- What did work well was sticking at things and not giving up when things were hard, or answers didn't come straight away.

"Those are the things we've got from looking back," said Ashar, "and if you don't stop and look, you often miss them, so well done for taking the time to do that. Now, whilst they are in your mind, we need to look forward because it's when the water going backwards meets the water coming forwards, that we make our wave." Alik came forward.

"You've noticed when looking back that Responsibility meant not making choices without thinking about their effect, and working together as a team," said Alik, "but, looking forwards, if we're going to keep the harbour nice for the future how can Responsibility help us?" Hands shot up everywhere – everyone knew the answer!

"Make good choices!" said one, and others followed up with what those choices might be like – 'not dropping litter', 'not putting fish bits in the harbour', and 'not dropping food scraps.'

"Knowing it takes all of us to help!" said another. There were loud cheers again!

"You've got it!" said Alik raising his fist in triumph in a manner most unlike him, "my work is done!"

Dante and Phoebe stepped forward laughing.

"The next 'looking forward' ingredient is Resilience," said Dante. "We were asked to get involved in this because no-one had managed to find a way to solve the problem of the harbour, it felt too hard, too big, and no-one by themselves felt up to the task."

"Too true!" shouted a voice, "but we did it!" Loud cheers again. Dante smiled; this was going to be easy too.

"So, Resilience means remembering that going forward," he said, "don't be put off because things seem hard, remember you have overcome problems before, and you can do it again. Believe you can bounce back, and you will; believe you are Resilient, and you will be." Phoebe stepped forward.

"Looking forward, also remember to be Resourceful," she said proudly, "you don't have to be Resilient by yourself. You might need several treasures to help you succeed, don't think you always have to do things by yourself, get the help you need!" There were cheers once again.

Clara stepped forward. "The truth is we have our wave when we let ourselves learn from looking back, and then look forward with confidence, and each other, knowing that between us we have, or can find, all the treasures we need."

There was a huge cheer, and the Mayor came to the front clapping. As the noise died down, he nodded at Solomon and the others who slipped out to the kitchen.

"It's time for my Thank You!" he said. "I know you're all expecting a long speech, but I'm going to disappoint you!" There was a loud cheer and he laughed but raised his hand to quieten them. "I know you're happy but hold your cheering for a moment please" he said, wanting to finish.

"I know we all want to thank our Positive Pirate team for showing us what real treasures are," he continued, "but you all deserve a Thank You for all the hard work you've put into making our harbour one to be proud of. There only really seemed one way to celebrate all we've achieved ... we had to have an actual Harbour Cake and here it is!"

Solomon and the team wheeled out a huge cake in the shape of the harbour – with the walls, the seafront, and the lighthouse proudly on show... but all around it were lots of little cakes, each with a wave on the top. It looked amazing.

There was silence for a moment as everyone took it in – then the biggest cheer you ever heard broke out and there was almost a riot – everyone wanted to taste a piece of Harbour Cake. Thankfully, there were more little cakes out the back so there was plenty to go around.

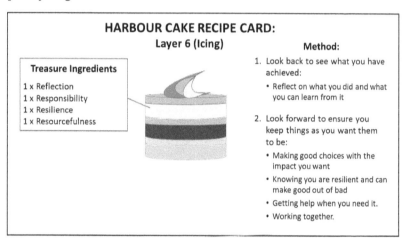

HARBOUR CAKE RECIPE CARD:
Layer 6 (Icing)

Treasure Ingredients

1 x Reflection
1 x Responsibility
1 x Resilience
1 x Resourcefulness

Method:

1. Look back to see what you have achieved:
   • Reflect on what you did and what you can learn from it

2. Look forward to ensure you keep things as you want them to be:
   • Making good choices with the impact you want
   • Knowing you are resilient and can make good out of bad
   • Getting help when you need it.
   • Working together.

Chapter 28: Afters or Starters

The Harbour Project celebration could not have gone better, and the Harbour Cake was the talk of the town. At the end of the celebration itself, Solomon had had all three of the bakers in town asking him to give them the recipe for the special three-layered cake, which had different flavours in each layer. They were keen to start making and selling 'wave cakes' as soon as possible.

Solomon had agreed with the Mayor that they would keep the recipe a Waterside secret so Solomon had given him the recipe to look after; the bakers would have to sign a document to promise that they would not share the recipe with anyone, and that they would only be made in Waterside.

Sunday was a day for clearing up as, of course, having spent so much time getting the harbour cleaned up, the last thing anyone wanted was for it to be left a mess after their celebration. The number of people helping with the clean-up of the harbour and the town hall, was increased by the promise that the few left-over wave cakes would be shared between those who joined in.

By late afternoon it was done. The Mayor was so grateful for all their help that he surprised the team by giving them a box with the last few remaining Harbour Cakes as a thank you – it surprised them as they thought they'd given them all away, but clearly the Mayor had secretly nabbed a few.

The team decided to go back to the ship for a rest and to eat their cake, as their own celebration of how well it had all gone.

"I think we can say our plan was a complete success!" said Clara, "I'm so proud of you all."

"Yes," agreed Phoebe, "I think our idea of using the Harbour Project to help them understand what treasures really are, worked brilliantly."

"We've been a great team," said Alik, "well, really the whole town has been!"

"And that cake was really delicious Solomon," added Rocco, who'd eaten his extremely quickly, and was hoping there was more.

"The work on the ship is going well too," said Clara, "they tell me it should be done in a couple more weeks, so at last we can start thinking about being Positive Pirates who actually sail the seas!"

"Finally!" said Phoebe excitedly. "So, can we start planning the naming ceremony too? Alik and I had lots of ideas about what we could do and there won't be any problem getting the Mayor to help us now." Clara nodded happily.

"Great," said Solomon, "don't forget, we're going to use that to ask people to help us with the other things we want to do to adapt the ship once the repairs are done. Ashar and I had some ideas about how we come up with that list, but it'll take a few days, so we need to get going on it."

"Yes, we will," agreed Clara. "My dad has offered to pay for the ship's name plate, and he's found someone to make it, and Mary's said she'll make the flag. I hope you've still got your designs Dante?"

"I certainly have," said Dante, "I'll make sure they get what they need."

"Excellent," said Clara, "so, tomorrow we start getting ready to set sail!"

"At last!" said Rocco, "is there any more cake to celebrate?"

There wasn't, but nobody really cared; their adventure was becoming a reality at last, and they couldn't have been happier.

Acknowledgements

There are a number of people who have helped me in the development of this book and to whom I want to say a big 'Thank You!'

Waterside Primary School, and particularly Emma Moakes (the Head Teacher), for the opportunity to develop this concept. I have very much appreciated their willingness to work with me on this and try out the approach of using these stories as part of a values-based curriculum.

Thank you too, to the following children from Waterside Primary School who have read the story and given me feedback, which was very encouraging and helpful:

- Amaya Andrews
- Kai Milsom
- Kaitlyn Andrews
- Kyrie Spears
- Maria Spacagna
- Oscar Gurung
- Phoebe Glaire
- Scarlett McEwing
- William Cowin

Thank you to Kate and Nick Mellor, who put me in touch with Emma and started this journey.

Thank you to my family and friends for all their help, encouragement, and support especially once I got to the point of taking the leap to publish.

A special thank you to my husband for proofreading and, along with my son, for the good-humoured challenge only they can provide, which has kept me from making some embarrassing trip-ups.

Last but not least, thank you to other authors, people I have never met, but who have dared to share their own questions, experiences, and insights about life. I have gained so much from their ability to stop, ask, feel, and listen that this has become a crucial part of my own journey. Through this process you have helped me to discover my own ability to make my ever-changing life a positive, fulfilling, and joyful experience and I am forever grateful.

Lightning Source UK Ltd.
Milton Keynes UK
UKHW020832070722
405464UK00006B/202